# MURDER BENIGN

Also by Richard Hunt

*Death of a Merry Widow*
*Deadlocked*

# MURDER BENIGN

## Richard Hunt

St. Martin's Press ≈ New York

Library of Congress Cataloging-in-Publication Data

Hunt, Richard
Murder benign / Richard Hunt.
p.    cm.
ISBN 0-312-14684-1
1. Police—England—Cambridge—Fiction.
2. Cambridge (England)—Fiction.    I. Title.
PR6058.U517M87    1996
823'.914—dc20    96-20015    CIP

First published in Great Britain by
Constable & Company Ltd

First U.S. Edition: October 1996

10   9   8   7   6   5   4   3   2   1

# 1

The accident happened, like most road accidents, because of a momentary lack of attention, and a fair slice of misfortune.

It was a glorious May morning when this particular driver's luck ran out. The sun wasn't in his eyes, so he should have seen the motor bike, before he pulled out on to a normally busy straight road.

It wasn't travelling all that fast, the motor bike, not for a Suzuki GS 500E, capable of speeds in excess of 110 mph.

The rider had no chance of getting out of the way, and the Suzuki hit the white Range Rover's front offside, at a slight angle.

The leather-clad rider's left knee caught the Rover's wheel arch, and the bike and rider parted company. The bike ended up on the grass verge, away down the road, while the rider slithered gracelessly to a halt in the drive of the bungalow opposite.

The rider's first reaction was to wrench off the red, visored crash helmet, loosing a confusion of long fair hair, and revealing a blue-eyed female face that would have been pretty, had it not been distorted by grimaces from the excruciating pain that surged through her body. Heart-rending high-pitched screams poured out of her wide-open mouth.

Pensioner George Norris, who was tinkering with his lawn mower in his open garage, reacted by dashing indoors and phoning 999.

Salesman Jimmy O'Neil, who was coming the other way, reacted by screeching his grey Vauxhall Cavalier to a halt. He was an alert intelligent young man and he quickly flicked on his hazard warning lights, grabbed his first-aid kit and dashed over to put into practice the lessons learned on his St John Ambulance course. His first job was to try and staunch the sluggish flow of blood from the torn leathers of the girl's strangely twisted left leg.

As is often the way of these things, by the time officialdom arrived in the form of Police Constable Withers from panda car D25, there was already a crowd of a dozen or more spectators standing about watching the proceedings with a curiously morbid interest.

'Come on. Move back now. Let's have some room,' PC Withers ordered.

'Her leg's bust, good and proper,' Jimmy O'Neil pronounced seriously, looking up momentarily from his kneeling position beside the patient. 'Her back might be broken too, so we mustn't move her.'

PC Withers nodded wisely, glad there were no vital decisions for him to make. He could confine his administrations to merely holding the girl's head still.

Her shrill gasping screams had died away into soft groans and moans.

'You'll be all right when the ambulance gets here,' Withers said comfortingly. 'What's your name, love?'

The question must have penetrated the waves of pain, for the girl suddenly stopped groaning and her blue eyes turned slowly in their tears until only the whites showed.

'Christ!' Withers muttered under his breath, fearing that he was witnessing the girl's demise.

Then she spoke, or rather, she croaked hoarsely, 'Samantha. Samantha Leverington. Tell my mum, please. 25 Ovingham Drive, Cherryhinton.'

'Take it easy, copper,' O'Neil growled anxiously. 'Keep your questions till later. Where the hell's that bloody ambulance?'

That bloody ambulance was doing its best, but it could make its way through the now congested road traffic no faster than it did.

To its paramedics, accidents like this were commonplace,

and they set about their work with all the confidence of much practice. Within a very short time the girl was securely strapped to a stretcher, in the ambulance, and on her way to the Accident and Emergency Department of Addenbrooke's Hospital in Cambridge.

With the accident victim now safely out of the way, PC Withers still had things to do. He quickly paced out the skid marks on the road and sketched a rough plan of the area in his notebook. The white Range Rover had sustained only superficial damage, so that could be moved over on to the grass verge. The motor bike was in no one's way where it was, and since there was no broken glass to sweep up, he could get the impatient traffic moving again.

Now all he had to do was to collect statements from those who had witnessed the accident.

Pensioner George Norris felt sorry for the injured young rider, so he stated categorically that he'd seen the white Range Rover pull straight out on to the main road in front of the motor cycle. That certainly was what had happened, but he was telling a lie, since he'd been tinkering with his lawn mower at the time.

Jimmy O'Neil had seen what had happened, but he'd been quite some distance away, and couldn't be all that positive.

The uninjured but distraught driver of the Range Rover had spent most of the time since the impact slumped uselessly in his car seat, with his head held between his hands. Now, standing unsteadily by the roadside, he was unnaturally pale, and his obvious attempt to try and pull himself together was only partially succeeding, since his hands were trembling.

'I really am sorry,' he muttered several times while wringing the fingers of those hands together in agitation. 'I just didn't see her.'

'You didn't see her . . .' PC Withers repeated as he wrote slowly on a fresh page in his notebook. 'What's your name and address – sir?'

'Me? I'm Sir Gordon Methuen Lignum, of The Willows,

Hansard Way, Newnham, Cambridge,' the driver replied hesitantly.

'Sir? You mean "Sir" as in "Order of the Bath" or "Knight of the Realm"?' Withers asked suspiciously.

'Baronet, actually.'

'I see – and your occupation?'

'I'm an archaeologist.'

'Ark-e-ol-o-gist,' PC Withers wrote laboriously.

'Look, will we be much longer?' Sir Gordon Lignum asked, looking at his watch and now showing signs of anxiety, or impatience. 'I'm supposed to have met some people ten minutes ago.'

'All in good time, sir. All in good time. Just a few more questions and we'll get your statement written out properly, then you can sign it.'

There was no need for Police Constable Withers to hurry. In a few hours he would be off duty, for a whole fortnight, with all the delights, sunshine and bars of the island of Malaga to look forward to.


Sir Gordon Lignum drove the Range Rover slowly and with extreme care along the rutted track that led to the excavation site.

The uncontrollable shivering and trembling of his limbs seemed to have settled down at last, but that tight feeling of sickness in the pit of his stomach was still there.

It had been there for several days in fact. Ever since he'd gone to see his doctor about that lump that had appeared in his neck.

The doctor had had no apparent doubt about what it was, and had not delayed in getting a sample of the offending tissue sent off to the hospital laboratory for analysis. The chances were, the doctor had said complacently, that the tumour would turn out to be benign. Its removal would then require only a minor operation. If it were malignant, though, his chances of living a long life were still good. Chemotherapy treatment of cancer had a good success rate nowadays, provided the tumour was caught in its early stages. He should not worry himself unduly.

Sir Gordon Lignum felt himself tense up again. It was all very well for his doctor to talk like that, it wasn't him with the problem. What if it was malignant? Those doctors would move a damned sight faster if they'd got the blasted thing, he thought angrily. Even now the spores of the tumour might be coursing round in his bloodstream, seeking to colonise his kidneys, his brain and all his other vital organs. In a few months' time it might be him lying on his back writhing and screaming in pain and agony, just like that poor girl he'd knocked off her bike had been, only in his case it would not be because of a few minor broken bones, but because the cancerous growths were devouring him from within. The very thought made him want to scream and lash out violently at this callously indifferent world of normal healthy humans.

He should have stayed at home, where he could wallow in his misery out of the sight of other people, but with Professor Gladsbury and Charles Choosely both away, he'd really had no choice. The site developers were paying the University good hard cash for this exploratory archaeological excavation, and the meeting with them to review progress had been one that he'd felt unable to put off.

He parked the Range Rover and looked round at the motley collection of other more elderly cars, then his fists pounded violently on the steering wheel like a denied spoiled child in a tantrum. He'd made the effort to get here, he'd undertaken that horrendous journey, albeit arriving some twenty minutes late, only to find that the developers were even later – they were still not here.

He got out and stood staring round the site with blind, angry, unappreciative eyes. Which was a pity, for the sun blazed down from a cloudless blue sky, making all the various colours on this piece of England's green and pleasant land radiate with an intensely vivid Mediterranean richness, and that was something that couldn't be said too often.

This particular piece of pleasant land, ready and ripe for development and undergoing exploratory archaeological

9

surgery, was a remote part of Hinching Park, not far from Huntingdon.

The turf and topsoil had been removed from several areas and taken away to distant spoil heaps, and the subsequent excavations had left a few skeletal raised patterns of straight lines, which indicated to the knowing eye the foundation walls of ancient buildings.

As Sir Gordon watched, the young students crouched or knelt at their work, searching diligently and methodically for the remnants of past lives, for the surviving bits and pieces of possessions, utensils and tools. It was a painstakingly slow process, according to the carefully restrained way most of them operated. However, near the wooden site hut were a small group of girls who were more physically active. They were working at a trestle table containing sieves, energetically riddling barrow loads of loose spoil, and carefully scanning the items held by the fine mesh for what others might have missed.

Suddenly one of those girls dropped her sieve and screamed loudly and shrilly. She jerked away from the table so convulsively that she fell over backwards – her feet knocked away a trestle and the whole apparatus collapsed to the ground.

Anxious concern was shown by some of those who quickly gathered round, but others burst into youthful laughter.

'What the hell's going on?' Sir Gordon snapped irritably as he strode over.

'I'm sorry, sir,' the girl said contritely and with some embarrassment as she got back to her feet, 'there was this thing in the soil. It suddenly appeared as I shook it.' She tentatively held up a large plastic tarantula by one of its long hairy legs. 'Ugh! I hate spiders!' She grimaced with a shiver, then tossed the child's toy away over her shoulder.

'Who put that stupid thing in there?' Sir Gordon roared, his pale drawn face becoming blotchily red with anger. 'Look at all this mess, and that's the batch I wanted fine-sieved for the flotation separator. For pity's sake, you lot are supposed to be the brightest out of your age group; God knows what the rest of them must be like, for I don't. A class of five-year-olds would have more sense. Which empty-headed idiot put that stupid thing in the sieves? Come on now! Who was it?' he shouted furiously at the small crowd that had now gathered round.

There was an embarrassed silence. Then a tall, broad-shouldered reddish-haired young man took a few steps forward, away from the others. His face was seriously calm, but his pale blue eyes looked cautiously wary.

'I put the spider in the sieve, Sir Gordon,' he admitted in a voice lilted lightly with a Scottish accent. 'I did not, of course, anticipate such a reaction as this, and I apologise . . .'

'You apologise! You apologise, do you, MacGregor?' Sir Gordon snapped out sarcastically. He was clenching his fists tightly. One inner voice was telling himself to get his anger under control, while another was asking just why the hell he should bother. 'I should bloody well think you do apologise,' he went on, a little more calmly. 'You're a third-year student. You're supposed to set an example to these others. Well, I've just about had enough of this kind of infantile humour. Archaeology is a serious business, and there's no place for practical joking on a site. It's got to stop. Do you hear me? I won't stand for it.' He glared round, but there were no eyes prepared to face him out. Most of his listeners appeared to be aimlessly studying the ground, or frowning at their fingernails. They were wondering how a usually mild man like him could suddenly have become so unpleasant. However, such apparent signs of humility effectively dulled the tirade.

'Right! Get back to work, all of you. Get this trestle set up again and clear this mess away, and no more nonsense.'

The chastened group dispersed soberly to their various places on the site.

Melissa Fairbrother walked down the slope to the bottom of exploratory trench 'K'. She picked up her pointing trowel and paintbrush and knelt down on her cushion. There could be no better way of spending such a lovely day as this than by being on one's hands and knees, gently and patiently probing and brushing away the years of soil deposits, looking for signs of long-dead humans.

Not that any of those long-dead humans would have been her ancestors, not here in these latitudes. There was about as much chance of that as of anyone looking at her and guessing that her name was Fairbrother, for Melissa's skin was a cool rich African bronze, and, of course, she was a woman, and brother to none.

Nothing wildly exciting had come to light in her trench so far. Only some carbonised material in a layer four feet or so down, which might, or might not, be the site of an ancient hearth or camp fire. Samples of that had been sent away for radio-carbon dating.

She carefully used the point of her trowel to tweak out some tiny stones, which she then brushed gently into her blue plastic dustpan.

'Maybe a midden; or a grave; a sherd, a bone or just a stone', she sang softly to herself as she worked.

Ten minutes later what had started to appear under her trowel and brush seemed, at first, to be a bone. It was pinkishly white, smooth and slightly rounded. Then she decided it might be a heavily patinated stone, perhaps a once brightly polished neolithic hand axe, although that would be unexpected in such a place and at such a level.

The stiff hairs of her brush cleared the dirt from some tiny little marks and indentations. As she brushed harder, more appeared. Then rows and rows of them.

Melissa's heart beat faster, and she sat back on her heels to survey the still half-embedded item. She shook her head vigorously from side to side in bewilderment and disbelief at what she saw. This was a find indeed, a real find.

'Tiny!' she screamed, as she jumped to her feet, waving her arms wildly. She was tall enough for her head and shoulders to appear above the top of the trench. 'Tiny! Come here! Quick!'

The tall, reddish-haired MacGregor walked towards her from a nearby square.

'What's up, Mel?' he asked calmly, his face still serious from his recent public dressing-down.

That expression changed to one of surprise when he bent down to study Melissa's find.

'I don't believe it,' he muttered to himself, reaching for the trowel, and proceeding to scrape away more of the enclosing soil. Then he stood upright. 'But it definitely is what it appears to be. Leave things just as they are, Melissa. I'll go and get Sir Gordon. Mark its position on the trench plan. Where is it? In the ninth metre from the datum line? Good, now locate its depth on the chart. Right, take a couple of photographs, then you can start sketching it.'

Sir Gordon was looking irritably at his watch, still waiting for the developers to arrive, when MacGregor called to him.

'It's probably just a bit of pottery,' he said offhandedly as they walked together to trench 'K', but he too shook his head in puzzlement as he crouched down over Melissa's find. He picked up the trowel and completed the disinterment of the clay tablet, with its neat rows of ancient cuneiform writing. Then he stood up and stared even more intently at what he held in his hands. His face started to redden again and his fingers clenched white in anger.

'Is this your idea of a joke? It's you again, MacGregor,' he yelled wildly, pointing an accusing finger at the young man. Then Sir Gordon Lignum lost control of his temper completely. 'You and your bloody stupid jokes!' he screamed. 'Well, you've gone too far this time. I'll have you sent down, by God I will. And this bloody black-skinned friend of yours too. This is no joke. A plastic spider's one thing, but this is a genuine artefact. Putting it here is tantamount to salting the site. For Christ's sake, there's no worse crime in my book.' He suddenly stopped waving his arms about, since he needed both hands to press against his chest, where his heart was pounding so hard it seemed it might burst. He breathed in deeply for a few moments. When he spoke again it was in a hoarse husky voice.

'You two are both suspended from lectures. Go on, get your gear and clear off this site. You won't be back, I can assure you of that. The rest of you, put the covers on this trench. No one's to work in it until I give the order. Right!'

Sir Gordon did not, however, wait to see that his instructions were carried out. He turned and strode off, still clutching the fragment of clay tablet.

He did not observe the two grey-suited businessmen from the London site developers who had just arrived in their green Jaguar, even though he passed within a few feet of them. He wrenched open the door of the Range Rover and fastened his seat belt with hands that still trembled, then he roared off, rather erratically, down the track.

At the junction with the main road he definitely glanced both ways, but there was nothing coming this time when he pulled out.

Somehow he managed to complete the drive to his home in Cambridge without incident. There he went into his study and sat down at his desk with his head in his hands. One finger roamed over that lump in his neck, and the unhappy, distraught man burst into tears.

It had certainly become a dreadful day for him, but it had also become a dreadful day for others whom fate had so unkindly thrown in his path.


The surgeons of Addenbrooke's Hospital were at work on one of those, the rider of the motor bike.

Samantha Leverington's injuries were bad, but not life-threatening. Her left hip had been dislocated, and had broken away part of its pelvic socket. That leg, below the knee, had multiple fractures, with a great deal of splintering. It was the removal of this splintered bone debris which took up much of the initial four-hour operation.

So it was that the next morning, a drowsy Samantha, propped up in bed on a miscellany of pillows, could start to reflect on the incident that had so dramatically and painfully affected her life.

Her left leg now lay in a shallow canvas hammock, which was attached to the strings, pulleys and weights that would keep her hip in traction for the next six to seven weeks. That leg, below the knee, was held together by a fixator – a contraption of metal bars to which were clamped the stainless steel pins which passed through the various pieces of her broken bones, and held them in some sort of alignment.

An anxious mother spent most of that first day with her, trying to console her daughter and at the same time divert her mind from the depths of the depression that had so understandably overwhelmed her.

The visit by the consultant who had operated did not help that process at all.

'I spend a lot of my time putting you motor cyclists back together again,' he said cheerfully, smiling as much for the benefit of his hovering attendant staff as for his patient.

'But it wasn't my fault,' Samantha protested.

'It very seldom is,' he went on. 'I think I'll be able to save your leg, but so much of the bone was shattered that your left shin is now about an inch shorter than the other one. The pieces should grow together in time, but you may still end up with one leg slightly shorter than the other. It's your hip that worries me at the moment. If that broken piece of your pelvic socket doesn't knit back properly, I might have to fit you with an artificial hip joint instead. How long will all this be necessary?' He waved a casual hand towards the fixator, the strings and the weights. 'You'll be in traction for at least six weeks, perhaps longer, but in three or four months you ought to be starting to hobble about on crutches. That tube in your arm is drip-feeding you with antibiotics. We don't want gangrene to set in, do we?'

No amount of drugs or medication could help the normally active Samantha come to terms with the prospect of being confined to a bed for a couple of days, let alone three or four months, and the next twenty-four hours saw frequent periods of petulance, anger and tears.

Her husband, Mark, just returned from rock climbing in Cumbria, came to visit, but his expressions of love, concern and sympathy were so intermingled with recriminations about her riding motor bikes that were much too powerful,

15

that she actually sighed with relief when at last he took himself off, back to their matrimonial residence in Huntingdon.

Cambridge, however, was her home town, and soon the news of her accident permeated through to old school friends. Visiting hours became enlivened with gossipy chats about events long past and almost forgotten, which, for a time at least, enabled her to forget her pain and discomfort.

More recent acquaintances dropped in as well. Pensioner George Norris visited, by coincidence, at the same time as salesman, Jimmy O'Neil.

'Lignum, his name was, and he's a Sir, would you believe?' Norris announced gruffly. 'He said he didn't see you. That's as good as admitting he was in the wrong.'

'That's right,' O'Neil added, 'and there was a "Halt" sign at that junction. He pulled out without stopping, so the police'll have him for dangerous driving, you mark my words.'

'The copper's name was Withers – I asked him,' Norris went on proudly. 'Thousands of pounds compensation you'll get, besides the insurance on your bike.'

'I'm not bothered about the money, but was my bike badly damaged? I haven't had it long. What's happened to it?' Samantha asked anxiously.

'Weren't much wrong with it,' Norris said. 'Stennard's Garage took it away. Mighty powerful bike for a young girl to be riding, young Stennard said. He reckoned it would be as much as he could do to handle it, and he's a big strapping fellow.'

'I do love my bike,' Samantha announced ruefully, 'and my leathers were ruined. They had to cut them off me, you see.'

'You can always get some more out of your compensation,' Norris suggested helpfully.

The succession of male visitors presented her with a problem of simple modesty.

'With one leg stuck up in the air like this, and having to keep the other one moving, all I can do is tuck my nightie between

16

my legs,' she explained to her mother. 'I can't get any knickers on, not with that thing on my leg.'

'Yes,' her mum said, nodding understandingly. 'I've been talking to the woman in the bed in the corner. She had the same problem. She's cut one leg of her knickers, and sewn on some press studs. I'll buy some new ones for you tomorrow, and do the same. Then you'll be all right.'

With modesty thus under some sort of control she began to look forward even more to visiting times.

It was during one of these periods, in the afternoon of her first Saturday, that her eyes suddenly lit up and her face beamed with pleasure. Three burly, booted, black-leather-clad visitors slowly approached her bed, each grinning broadly. Prominent on their sleeves were large brightly coloured club badges depicting a dog's head with bared vicious teeth. They carried a variety of gifts, get-well cards, fruit, flowers and motor-cycle magazines. The motor-cycle club committee had come to commiserate with its injured member.

Initially their faces showed anger as Samantha proudly related, in some detail, the full extent of her injuries, but when that necessity was over, the conversation quickly became that of the motor-cycle enthusiast, liberally interspersed with 'Suzuki this', 'Honda that' and the odd 'Kawasaki'.

Samantha's pretty face was soon transformed from its now accustomed melancholia into happy vivacity.

However garbed, these visitors – a lawyer, an accountant, and a butcher – were very socially aware people, and they did not ignore the other ladies in that ward. They had friendly words, smiles and good humour enough for all. Soon the whole place had a party atmosphere.

'So you've met up with one of the "Sorry, I didn't see you" brigade, Sammy. You'll get a purple heart badge for that, but it's not a very exclusive award, I'm afraid,' the lawyer said, smiling down at the radiant Samantha.

'This one's an archaeologist. Sir Gordon Lignum, no less, and he drove a Range Rover and lives near the river, in Newnham,' she said proudly.

'They come in all shapes and sizes.'

'They ought to be strung up by their whatsits from the nearest church steeple,' the butcher announced sternly, making the only acrimonious remark of the afternoon.

'There's not enough steeples for all of them,' one of the others replied.

The ward staff turned a blind eye to transgressions of visitors' rules, and even provided refreshments from the tea trolley, plus a little banter of their own. For these three leather-clad men were bright-eyed, and had charm. Samantha Leverington was not an easy patient; perhaps now things might improve.

Thus was the situation when Mark Leverington arrived. He was serious-faced from his drive in his safe and steady Volvo estate, and still anxious to bring his wife round to his view that riding fast motor bikes was not a suitable pastime for any young woman, and his wife in particular. Neither were the male members of such clubs the kind of society he wished her to mingle with. To find her obviously enjoying such company brought an additional surly glint to his eyes.

'Have the police been to see you yet?' he demanded. 'No? Why the devil not? My solicitor says it will be a great help if the police prosecute this Lignum fellow. I'm afraid he might claim it was your fault, because the bike was obviously far too big for you to handle.'

'Nonsense,' the butcher interposed scornfully. 'Sammy here's as good on her bike as any man. Why, she got first prize riding between the cones at the rally in Oxford last month.'

'I did, didn't I?' Samantha said, turning in relief to her champion. 'But that was only because you'd adjusted my chain to stop it snatching at low speed.'

'That's always been a problem with that model,' the lawyer added knowingly. 'I had the same sort of thing with my first Honda, but chains are always difficult, especially if there's a bit of wear.'

Mark Leverington found that he could hardly get a word in. Motor bikes didn't interest him and there was no chance to

18

turn this conversation round to the subject that did – rock climbing.

So the afternoon passed into evening, and eventually the visitors departed, minus their presents, leaving a tired but tearfully happy Samantha to reflect that outside the walls of her ward there was still a life to be led, and it was only a matter of time and patience, then she could be out there again to enjoy it.

That same evening Sir Gordon Lignum also had visitors, but one of his came armed, not with flowers, cards or other presents, but with an iron bar. An iron bar that was used to ruthlessly batter the archaeologist about the head, until he lay dying on the carpeted floor of his study.

That visitor quickly tore the written sheets from the writing pad on the desk, and put those, with the strange fragment of baked clay tablet containing its rows of neatly impressed cuneiform characters, into a large holdall. To those things were added many of the small apparently valuable items found on a quick tour of the other rooms, mostly jewellery, porcelain and silver.

Then the visitor left, through the same unlocked french window at the rear of the house by which entry had been made.

An hour or so later, the dead man's wife, Lady Ingrid Lignum, arrived home from rehearsing the choral section of Beethoven's Ninth Symphony, due to be performed early the following month in the city's Guildhall.

White and shaken by the sight of her husband's battered body, she nevertheless managed a hesitant yet competent 999 call to summon the police. An ambulance clearly wasn't needed.

Before the police arrived, however, it was necessary for her to go into the sitting-room and pour a stiff gin into a cut crystal tumbler, to which she added only a minuscule amount of tonic. That didn't last long, so it was followed quickly by another, and yet another.

# 2

Detective Chief Inspector Sidney Walsh was a broad-shouldered man, about six feet tall, with the greying streaks in his dark brown hair appropriate for one in his early fifties. Although his eyes were keen and shrewd in a somewhat serious face, yet there was a hint of humour in his features, as well as stubborn determination.

He was working in the spare double bedroom when the telephone rang.

He'd stripped the old wallpaper off during the morning, and after lunch had put the first coat of thick white emulsion on the ceiling. However, for his wife Gwen, that one coat was not enough, and a second was needed.

Walsh was phlegmatic about such things. In his opinion the room hadn't really needed decorating anyway, but some American friends of Gwen's were coming to England shortly, and naturally they had been invited to come to Cambridge and stay for a few days, so of course that room had to be redecorated and have new curtains; there was no point in arguing about it.

Walsh was the head of the Cambridgeshire Constabulary's serious crime team, so the telephoned message about a suspected murder was very much his business; nevertheless he finished giving that ceiling its second coat and rinsed the brush clean before setting off.

Gwen, dark-haired and slender, her bottom lip nipped between her teeth in intense concentration, was carefully painting round the window frame with white gloss, when he went to kiss her goodbye.

There had been no great need for Walsh to hurry to the scene of the crime, because the forensic team leader, Dr Richard

Packstone, a tall, rather cadaverous-looking grey-haired man in his sixties, would assume command of the situation there, as was his right and duty, for the collection and preservation of evidence was his responsibility.

So when Sidney Walsh did eventually arrive he could afford to spend a few moments just standing in the drive of the house in Newnham, looking round and getting his bearings.

It was a spacious, red-brick, modern house, with two white-painted columns supporting a small triangular roof over the front door. A neatly lawned front garden was kept private from the road by a high trimmed laurel hedge. The driveway itself was surfaced with herringbone patterned brick, as was the passage through the side gate to the rear of the house, and the wide patio at the back.

Dr Packstone greeted Walsh on that patio, outside an aluminium-framed sliding french window.

'The body's in a study at the end of the house there,' he said impassively. 'The only door to it is from this lounge. The doctor will be here in a minute, but you can come in if you like.'

Walsh donned an all-enveloping plastic dungaree suit and pulled an elasticated washerwoman's hat on his head before entering. They would effectively prevent the scene of the crime becoming contaminated with any of Walsh's fallen hairs or other body debris.

'He's not a pretty sight, is he?' Walsh muttered, more to himself than to any of the others, as he crouched down by the mortal remains of Sir Gordon Lignum.

The body lay partly on its side with its knees bent, before an old brown leather-topped mahogany desk with tarnished brass drawer handles. An upholstered swivel chair lay on its side close by.

The body was dressed in a dark blue sweater, black corduroy trousers, black socks and black shoes. The black emphasised the paleness of the man's exposed skin. His face was hollow-cheeked and the jaw hung limply open to display the macabre grin of healthy white teeth. It was the reasonably good-looking face of a somewhat serious man in his middle to

21

late thirties. It was the back of his head which wasn't a pretty sight.

The doctor arrived, and Walsh stepped back out of the way.

'Well, this man's death was no accident, neither was it suicide,' the doctor said slowly while studying the man's neat fingernails, answering, if that were necessary, the two most important unasked questions, 'but I can't see anything to suggest that there was a fight, or even that he grappled with his killer.'

Richard Packstone shook his head slowly, even though he obviously agreed with the doctor's opinion. 'It rather looks as though he was sitting at his desk writing, when he was hit from behind. Then he would have slipped naturally off the chair into that position on the floor, but there were more blows than the one, I should think.'

'Probably, it's difficult to say, but the autopsy will sort that out,' the plump grey-suited doctor replied, pulling on the lower of his three chins. 'Certainly a heavy instrument was used, perhaps a hammer or a short length of iron bar. There's no sign of the weapon?'

'Not yet,' Packstone said.

'Time of death?' Walsh asked.

'He's been dead a couple of hours or so, maybe a bit less,' the doctor replied cautiously, then after a few moments' cogitation, he added, 'Say between eight and nine.'

Walsh nodded thoughtfully. There was no way of getting an absolutely precise time of death, even though the doctor, and the pathologist when he arrived, would do calculations based on the body's temperature and the temperature in the room, but the result would still be qualified to at least a half-hour, plus or minus. The doctor's experienced estimate was probably as accurate an answer as he would ever get.

So far he'd been concentrating on learning whatever he could from observation of the body; now it was time to take in the surrounding details.

Sir Gordon's study was what a woman might well describe as a 'man's room'. It had a brown carpet, thick velvet curtains of a similar shade, and walls covered with a heavily embossed paper – emulsioned in beige. Two large paintings hung on the long wall opposite the window. Walsh moved away from the others to study them. One was a scene of the storming of the Arapil Grande during Wellington's Peninsular battle at Salamanca, and the other of Nelson's *Victory* firing its first broadsides into the stern of the *Bucentaure* in the early stages of the Battle of Trafalgar. Both were in oils, on canvas, and looked contemporaneous, as far as he could judge, with the period they illustrated. The one of the *Victory*, however, was much darkened by age and grime, and in need of a good clean.

On the far wall was a large framed print of the massive stone walls of a ruined city, its central feature being a gateway guarded on either side by two leopardly looking carved stone lions. The copperplate writing of the title read, 'The Lion Gate, Hattusa, the capital city of the Hittite Empire, *circa* 1300 BC. Turkey. From an engraving by S. Lough, 1908'.

Beneath that hung something obviously very modern. It was a framed pencil-sketched portrait of a man, undoubtedly the man who now lay dead upon the floor. It was simple, yet very well done, since the artist had managed to capture some character in the face's expression. That man was a thinker, someone content to withdraw for long periods into an inner world of academic pondering and debate. Yet just a few subtle strokes of the artist's pencil about the eyes also suggested that this man could, on occasions, confront the outer world with a gentle humour and even affection. The drawing was entitled and signed, in neat copperplate handwriting, 'Gordon, by Ingrid'.

Also on the same wall hung a curved, rather rusty cavalry sword and two horse pistols, neither of which looked genuine, and with them a murderous-looking Irish shillelagh, which did.

'These things look pretty heavy, Richard. Could one of them have been used to bash this man's head in?' Walsh asked.

'Can't tell, not with the naked eye. That's laboratory work. We'll take them in when all the photography's done,' came the reply.

Walsh nodded wisely. It had been an unnecessary question, Packstone would never have missed anything so obvious. He turned his attention to the other things in the room, trying to record in his memory all the details, so that he would be able to recall them later in his mind, and study them at his leisure.

He'd noticed before in such situations that the effort of concentration keyed up his senses to the point where he felt he was also trying to absorb the mystic atmosphere of the place. If the spirit of the dead man wished to pass on a message, his mind was tuned in to receive it. Any tip or clue would come in handy. It was a pity that no murder victim he'd ever come up against had communicated anything that way; it would have made his life a lot easier.

On the desk were some open books and a thick A4 lined writing pad, the top sheet of which was blank. A massive bookcase took up nearly the whole of the wall behind the door. Two-thirds of its shelves held close-packed volumes; the rest of the space held an untidy collection of broken pottery sherds and stone artefacts. On the floor, in the corner near the window, was a small old-fashioned combination safe, next to which, rather incongruously, was a large television on a stand and under it a CD player. The green light on that CD player was still glowing.

'What was being played, and how high was the volume?' Walsh asked, pointing at the instrument. It was not for him to go poking about pressing buttons at the scene of a crime, not until he was sure Forensic had completed all their finger-printing tests and examinations.

'Beethoven's Ninth. Berlin Philharmonic,' Packstone replied, promptly going over and pressing a button. From the twin speakers came the sounds of the orchestra playing the first part of the first movement, not blaringly loud but quite enough to blot out the sounds a stealthy murderer might have made.

'Mrs, I mean, Lady Lignum had taken herself off to bed before I arrived. What did she have to say?' he asked.

'Not a lot,' Packstone replied with a wry grin. 'Whether she'd been drinking before she came home, I don't know, but if she hadn't, she certainly made up for it later. She told us that she'd seen no one hanging about outside, and that most of her jewellery's disappeared from her bedroom, and so have some silver and porcelain pieces from other rooms. Then her doctor arrived, and decided she was in a state of post-traumatic shock. He gave her a hefty sedative and made her go to bed. You won't hear a peep out of her for a long while.'

That was a pity. Talking to the murdered man's wife would obviously have been the best way to start an investigation, but in cases of sudden death the next of kin usually needed time to get over the initial shock of their loss before they were ready to think and talk rationally.

'The top sheet of that pad on the desk, is there any indication of what he was writing?' Walsh wanted to know.

'George, have you done the desk top yet?' Packstone asked one of his assistants. There was a shake of the head. 'Do the pad then, would you please?'

The black graphite dust wiped lightly over the surface of the page highlighted the impressions left when the sheet above had been written on. Walsh leaned over to read it.

'. . . more such pottery fragments were found in the midden in the same section. This kind of coarse ware is common in such locations, and was probably fired from local clays for local use. The decorative patterns though, such as they are, are unusual, consisting of regular patterns of impressed short straight lines, not unlike repetitive letters in cuneiform . . .' There the neat writing ended; further down the page 'B9' and 'K9' had been written, but these were in wild and loopy characters, as though they were mere doodles, done while the mind was deeply engrossed in other matters. They had each been ringed with round-cornered oblongs, rather like the Egyptian cartouches which enclose hieroglyphs of royal names, and, as if that were not emphatic enough, they had been underlined twice as well.

Walsh shrugged his shoulders and gave a last quick glance round the room. He felt he'd missed nothing of importance, but he could refresh his memory later, when Forensic had

25

finished and the body had been taken away. There would also be plenty of photographs to peruse. The place was still dead to ethereal emotions. No hate, no love, no bitterness – nothing.

It was time to move on and leave Packstone and his team to finish their work uninterrupted. Perhaps Sir Gordon's killer had left some signs of his passing outside. He'd go and see.

Waiting on the patio, Walsh found the two other members of his serious crime team.

Detective Sergeant Reginald Finch sat on a cast-iron garden chair. He had a lean pale face with a somewhat prominent beaky nose, blue eyes and fair hair. Tall and lanky, in his early thirties, he was married to a social worker, and had a wide interest in most things historical, and a specific interest in the well-being of the occupants of a nearby home for young handicapped orphans, which was where he'd been earlier that evening, with his wife, organising a mini-disco.

Detective Constable Brenda Phipps, however, paced restlessly up and down. She was of average height, slender, in her late twenties, and very pretty. Her bright eyes were brown, as was her unruly hair. Sometimes when she smiled, that prettiness dissolved away into sheer disarming love-liness. Keeping fit was one of her pleasures, but she combined that fitness with a skill and ability in the martial arts that had made her into one of the Constabulary's most deadly exponents of unarmed combat. Surprisingly in one so physi-cally active, she could also sit patiently for hours on end at her other hobby, that of restoring damaged and broken porcelain.

'They say the Lady's gone to bed as drunk as a lord, Chief,' Brenda Phipps announced brightly.

'Drowned her sorrows with gin, boss,' Reginald Finch added.

'So I gather,' Walsh replied, shrugging his shoulders. 'She must be drunk if she can sleep with all this lot banging about in her house.' Walsh looked down at his watch. 'It's a bit late. I can't see us getting much done this evening.'

'Do you mean to say we're not going to spend the next three

or four hours on our hands and knees crawling all over the lawns and through the dirtiest hedges and ditches you can find, looking for tracks and clues, Chief?' Brenda Phipps demanded, raising her eyebrows in mock surprise. 'We usually do. In fact I came prepared for it, I've got my oldest jeans on. You're not feeling ill by any chance, are you?'

'It's a nice night for a bit of fresh air, boss, and it's warm and dry, too,' Reg Finch chipped in with a smile.

They were baiting him, but it was in good humour, and that he did not mind. He knew, as they obviously did, that he had a liking for hands and knees tracking. As a Boy Scout, in his youth, he'd studied the paw prints of animals in muddied ground and had followed the passage of foxes, dogs and badgers. That natural boyish interest had been extended some years later when he was convalescing from broken ribs and a torn left ear, sustained in the only match in which he'd played when on a Lions rugby tour of Australia. He'd spent a memorable week with a lucid Aboriginal police tracker in the Western Australian deserts. From that wise man he'd learned the real power of reasoned observation. A few animal footprints could reveal not only the species and direction of movement, but probable age, weight, size and speed of travel. It was only a game to some, and of merely passing interest to others, but to Walsh it had been a fascinating insight into the world of true deduction, and one that had remained with him throughout the development of his career as an investigating police officer. The desertless tracts of Cambridgeshire provided few opportunities for a now almost deskbound departmental head to put any of this art into practice, but as his assistants' wry humour suggested, it was rare that he let any chance slip past, when one did arise.

He pulled thoughtfully at his left ear lobe, as though making sure the injury had properly healed. Tomorrow's daylight would obviously be the best time to look for traces of the killer's movements, and certainly a full search of the premises and grounds would be necessary to try and find the murder weapon, yet the sooner tracks were followed, if there were any, the better. Circumstances could so easily change, then

27

the opportunity might be lost for ever, and rain, the destroyer of tracks, was always a possibility.

'You're both quite right,' he said finally. 'We'll get torches and give the grounds as good a going-over as we can, while we can. We'll do along the back of the house here first.'

His words were greeted with broad grins.


The brick-weave patio had a rippling scalloped edge to the lawn, and the lights of the house illuminated the area so well that the two old-fashioned *Dixon of Dock Green* ex-street gaslamps, now converted to electricity – set, presumably to provide a muted or romantic light – merely glowed ineffectually.

The kitchen door was still locked on the inside but its casement window was hooked open. Just inside, on the windowsill, was a tall, narrow glass vase containing three bright yellow roses, one of which had shed some of its petals. They lay where they had fallen. Clearly that window had not been the way of entry or exit of the intruder. The next window was of the dining-room, which was closed, then came the french window of the sitting-room.

'Forensic have found prints on that door handle, Chief,' Brenda Phipps announced, 'but there are smudges which suggest that whoever touched them last wore gloves.'

Walsh nodded. 'If the front and side doors were locked then Lignum's killer must have gone in that way. What we need to find out is whether he came into the garden from the back, or round from the front of the house.'

'True,' Reg Finch added thoughtfully, 'but how did he know this french window would be open? If the murderer had prior knowledge of that, then this killing must have been premeditated and planned, and not the result of excessive violence from a petty sneak thief, as I think we're supposed to believe.'

'For crying out loud, Reg,' Brenda protested scornfully. 'We've only just started this case. We know next to nothing yet, and you want to start speculating already?'

'You were just thinking out loud, weren't you, Reg?' Walsh

said hastily. 'Plenty of time for that later. Come on, let's see if there's any way of access into the back garden.'

Away from the house there was more light than was at first apparent. Some of it came from the distant rosy glow of the city, over the tall trees at the end of the garden, but that was augmented by occasional showings of the moon through the gaps in the invisible clouds. The breeze was mild and pleasant, particularly after the heat of the day.

A high board fence stood firm and solid behind the bushy verdant shrubs in the flower beds that ran down each side of the wide lawn. The concentration of torchlight showed that even in the rare gaps there were no signs of the disturbance and trampling that would have occurred had someone clambered over from the grounds of the houses to either side.

As they neared the end of the garden the lawn suddenly sloped downwards quite dramatically, then levelled off again, probably as much as three or four feet lower. The branches of the trees blocked out any moonlight, and so it seemed much darker, and the air was still and heavy with the dank sweet smell of river water. The ground became distinctly softer underfoot.

Those trees did not grow in the garden itself, for the lawn just petered out into a bankless stream or ditch some four or five feet wide. On the far side, on a long narrow eyot or island, grew the trees and a tangle of shrubs. Beyond them the torches illuminated patches of water that could only be the slow-moving, turgid River Cam.

Here was an entry point wide enough to admit an army marching in column, if such were prepared to swim or wade the liquid barrier, but it was not with that possibility in mind that Walsh shone his torch over the softer ground and the grassy shallows. There were marks and indentations but he ventured no comment on them as he worked his way along the water's edge. So dark was it, and so intent was he on the area illuminated by his torch, that when he came to something more substantial than mud and water, he nearly tripped over it. It was the platform end of a punt, grounded on the edge of the lawn, close up against the shrubs which had continued when the fence had ended and to one of which a mooring rope had been loosely tied. The rest of the punt lay at an angle across the ditch, with its far end on the island, opposite the garden of the house next door. It was an old punt, with silver flaking varnish, and it lacked a pole, a paddle, or cushions, probably because it was half full of water.

'No problem for anyone coming in this way, Chief,' Brenda ventured, waving her torch in the direction of the river and the island.

'True!' Walsh replied, with a slight sound of despondency in his voice. 'But I'm afraid I can't confirm whether anyone has actually done so lately. This ground here is far too spongy to hold any light impressions for long,' he explained, crouching down to press his fingers into the soggy ground. 'See,' he went on, but the other two had already lost interest.

'Listen! There's someone on a boat, out there on the river,' Reg said softly.

They heard the faint sounds of splashing and the low murmur of voices, followed by a girlish giggle.

'They might have seen something on their way upstream, Chief. I'll go and have a word with them,' Brenda announced positively. She stepped forward on to the punt's platform, then, with arms held wide for balance, started walking towards the island along the side of the boat, as though on a tightrope. Punts are quite stable craft, especially when grounded at both ends, yet it would have been surprising if such a journey could have been made without some movement, and that duly happened when Brenda had nearly completed her trip. The sudden lurch necessitated her reaching out for the firmer ground at least a half-stride too soon, and so her sandalled foot found a soft glutinous muddy patch, one inch deep in water.

'Yuk,' came Brenda's learned response as she grabbed at some of the overhanging branches to restore her balance.

The sounds she made as she forced her way through the tangled undergrowth of the narrow island, and the light from her wildly waving torch, created some surprise and even fear in one of the occupants of the vessel on the river.

A girl gave a low-pitched scream, which ended with the words, 'What is it?' indicating, presumably, that she feared the possible presence of some large wild predatory animal on the bank – complete with torch.

'Don't be afraid,' Brenda called out reassuringly. 'I'm a police officer. Can you pull over here to the bank? I'd like a word with you, if you don't mind.'

'Oh Lord,' groaned a male voice. 'I'm going to get booked for speeding, or paddling without due care and attention. I'll probably lose my licence. Can you grab that branch, Mel?'

The light from Brenda's torch illuminated a broad-shouldered young man seated on the platform at the back of the punt. His muscles rippled as he reached backwards and sideways to put in a powerful stroke with his paddle. He had a rugged face, a snub nose and wore white shorts and a white T-shirt with the word 'Tiny' printed in red letters across the chest.

The girl kneeling at the other end of the punt wore a loose black cotton dress, and her skin was much the same colour, so almost the only white to be seen was the white of her eyes, until she spoke and showed her teeth.

'Are you really a police officer?' she asked in a clear, precise and well-modulated voice.

'Nope! She's Mrs Crusoe, marooned on this lonely island by her mutinous crew,' Tiny suggested.

'A pirate's moll, more likely. Set up to do the sexy siren act and lure us into the clutches of her wicked gang who'll rob me of my jewels and ravish me – with a bit of luck,' Melissa laughed.

'There's been a break-in at the house up there,' Brenda announced mundanely – the mention of murder would be inappropriate under the circumstances. 'What time did you go upriver? Did you see anything suspicious along here as you went by?'

The two in the punt were silent for a few moments.

'We went by here between half-eight and nine, I'd say,' Tiny replied. 'It was getting quite dark, but I can't say I remember seeing anything in particular.'

31

'I saw a kayak canoe somewhere near here. A white one, I think it was,' the dark girl said hesitantly. 'There was a man in it. At least I'm pretty sure it was a man. He was wearing a black wet-suit or a leather jacket, but I didn't see his face, he kept his head turned away.'

'That's very good,' Brenda remarked, approvingly. 'I'd like statements from you both if – '

'There's three more boats still up near Grantchester. Maybe they'll have noticed something,' Melissa suggested.

'Chief! Did you hear that?' Brenda turned to shout to the mainland.

'I'm not deaf,' Walsh growled, his voice sounding strangely muted and unreal, coming from the darkness on the other side of the undergrowth.

'Are you in a hurry to get home?' Brenda asked the punt's occupants. 'Would you take me back upriver so that I can talk to those people, please?'

'Suits me,' Tiny said cheerfully. 'I've nothing of importance on tomorrow – in fact I've nothing much on now, come to think of it, but my modesty is sufficiently intact to receive lady visitors.'

'Never fear, I'll be here as chaperone. Otherwise you might easily fall into the arms of the law,' Mel responded lightly.

In spite of the ready wit and banter from these two, there was just the slightest hesitation in the way they spoke that suggested they were not quite as relaxed and at ease as it at first appeared, or so Brenda thought.

'I'll get back as soon as I can, Chief,' she called out.

By hanging on to the branches and leaning out as far as she could, she could just reach the front of the punt with the toe of her foot.

'Can you get in any closer?' Brenda asked.

'I'm doing my best,' Tiny said as he gave another vigorous stroke with the paddle. The punt came nearer the bank, but the current was starting to swing the boat round, threatening to take it sideways downstream. Brenda jumped and reached for Melissa's outstretched hand, but her leap did not carry her forward far enough, and she landed with a splash across the bows, her legs in the river.

The other two occupants exploded into whoops of laughter as Brenda clambered aboard.

'Are you all right, Brenda?' Walsh called anxiously.

'From the waist up I am, the rest of me's a trifle wet. Never mind, it's all in a day's work. My radio's still working at any rate,' she replied, a little more cheerfully than she actually felt.

'You ought to get those wet clothes off, Inspector Brenda,' Tiny suggested hopefully.

'If it wasn't so dark you'd see that was said with a lecherous grin,' Mel explained.

'There's a paddle down there somewhere, Superintendent Brenda. A bit of hard work and you'll soon dry out.'

'I'm a Detective Constable, actually.'

'Never mind, you can't all be Big Chief Constables, can you?'

The sounds of splashing could be heard by those on dry land, so presumably the punt was now back on its way upstream.

'Are you two undergraduates?' Walsh heard Brenda ask.

'Me – Churchill,' Melissa replied.

'Me – Downing,' Tiny said.

'Downing? That's good, you must know Professor Hughes then. He's a particular friend of mine.'

'Lord, she knows one of my tutors. It'll pour with rain any minute,' Tiny moaned.

'Good! That'll cool your ardour,' Melissa giggled.

The murmur of conversation started to fade into the distance.

'Come on, Reg. She'll be all right. She can look after herself,' Walsh said, turning away. 'Let's go and look round the front of the house.'


The brick-weave paving led round the side of the building and expanded to front the double garage, then looped out to the road.

'We've got statements from people in some of the houses down the road, sir, but there's still a few cars up the lane there that we haven't done,' announced the burly uniformed Sergeant Dobbs. 'I did wave down one that left a little while ago, and I took his name and address, in case you wanted to question him later.'

'What's up there, then?' Walsh demanded.

'That's Grantchester Meadows,' Dodds replied, as if surprised that anyone was not aware of the area of marshy grassland that edged the river for the few miles to the village of that name and its unreliable church clock, made famous by Rupert Brooke while he reminisced on the doubtful attractions of the local village girls of his day. It was an area popular with local lovers, particularly on a warm late spring evening – those that could be bothered to get out of their cars and walk in the moonlight.

Walsh looked at his watch again. Obviously it was possible that the occupants of those cars might have seen something when they'd passed Sir Gordon Lignum's house.

'Come on then. We'll check them out ourselves,' he said.

There were four cars parked close to the bushes on the muddy ground under the overhanging trees near the narrow entrance gate to the meadows beyond.

The first held no occupants, but those in the second took instant exception to Walsh shining a torch into their vehicle.

'Here, are you some kind of bloody queer or something?' a short stocky man, clad in a loose black track suit, shouted angrily, as he hurriedly climbed out of a rear door.

'Belt him one, Bert,' a shrill female voice suggested.

Bert needed no such instructions, for he was already swinging his right fist into a punch aimed at Walsh's face.

Walsh had to step back quickly to avoid the blow. 'Cut it out! I'm a police officer,' he snapped out sharply, then his feet slipped on the mud and he fell backwards on to the soft ground.

'And I'm the bleeding Queen of Sheba,' Bert yelled angrily, aiming a kick at Walsh's sprawling body, which fortunately missed.

'We are police officers,' Reg shouted, hurrying back from the third car. 'I warn you, you'll spend the rest of the night in the cells if you don't watch out.'

'Here, Bert, take it easy. If my hubby finds I've been with you again he'll bloody well kill me, he will,' the voice from within the car whispered loudly and insistently.

The arrival of Sergeant Dodds, in uniform, dispelled any of Bert's remaining doubts.

Walsh pushed himself to his feet, and bent to pick up his fallen torch. The bulb had broken and both his hands were dirty and gritty. He wiped them on the backside of his jeans, but that didn't help much since that area was even more muddy.

'How long have you two been here?' he demanded irritably.

'About half an hour,' Bert replied resentfully.

'You're no help to us then, but I tell you this, you'd better keep your temper under control in future, or you'll be in serious trouble,' Walsh growled angrily.

The damp was working its way through the denim of his jeans and it already felt distinctly uncomfortable. There was an old blanket in the boot of his car. He'd need to put that over the driver's seat before sitting down, or else he'd make a right mess of the car's cloth upholstery.

'T'weren't my fault. You should wear uniforms when you go nosing about, spying on decent people,' Bert responded sulkily.

The driver of the third car had come over to see what all the fuss was about.

'I can't say I saw anything, I'm afraid,' he offered in response to Reg's question, 'but there were several more cars here when we arrived. I remember that one of them was a grey Volvo, if that's any help.'


'We didn't learn a great deal from that, Reg,' Walsh said later, as they walked back to Lignum's house.

'It was a bit of a long shot,' Reg observed placidly.

'Brenda! Where are you now?' Walsh spoke into his radio.

'Hello, Chief. We're on our way back now. We couldn't find the back of the house in the dark, so I'm going down to the boat-yard at the Mill. Can someone pick me up there, do you think?' she asked.

'Reg'll do that. I'm going off home for a bath and a bit of shut-eye. I'll meet you both back here at eight tomorrow morning, or thereabouts.'

However the plans of mere mortals do so often gang awry, for it was at that moment that Sergeant Dodd's radio crackled into its combination of human gibberish and ether static. It was incomprehensible to anyone more than a yard away, yet to Dodds it was an urgent message.

'An intruder's been reported at a house two streets up there,' he said quickly, lengthening his stride and pointing in a westerly direction, away from the river. 'We're – that is, me – I'm the nearest.'

The significance of such a report was not lost on the two plain-clothed officers. An intruder had entered Sir Gordon Lignum's house, taking easily carried valuables and possibly killing the property owner into the bargain. This reported intruder might possibly be the same one, so his apprehension was vitally necessary.

'Get a move on then,' Walsh barked out as he started to run in the direction of Dodds's pointed finger. 'I don't know this area. Give us directions for heaven's sake.'

'Two streets up there on the right – Victoria Gardens – number 20,' Dodds snapped out readily enough. 'That's about half-way down on the far side. There's a back passage to the rear. You cover this end of it, Reg and I'll go round the far end. You'd better stay in the street, sir, and do the front of the house.'

Wise instructions, Walsh thought to himself. He, the eldest and most deskbound, was given the shortest distance to run – he was already being outpaced by the other two. It hadn't always been like that. In his younger days as a rugby back row forward, he'd been proud of the speed he could generate over short distances. He wasn't doing too badly even now. As he came into Victoria Gardens, though, he slowed down to a fast walking pace. On either side were terraced houses, with their front doors opening directly on to the pavement. Once these had been low-cost homes for workman and artisan; now they were ultra-modernised bijou dwellings for the Cambridge equivalent of the Docklands yuppie, judging by the value of many of the cars parked there.

Victoria Gardens was still and silent in the pale glow of the street lights as Walsh walked down it. He'd been asked to cover the least likely way of escape for the intruder, for such people preferred to slink along dark unlit back passages. Reg or Dodds had the best chance of making a capture.

Yet, half-way along that far side there was a gap in the row of houses. That might just be another passage linking up to the one that went along the back. He hurried towards it, and was nearly there when he heard a distant shout. It sounded like Dodds's voice. Then a dark figure came darting out of the gap.

Walsh leapt forward with arms outstretched to envelop the person in a smothering bear hug, but that figure had caught sight of him and with a high-pitched screech of fright shot off down the pavement. Walsh's leap turned into a despairing full-length dive. As his knees hit the ground his grasping fingers just managed to hook into the neckband of the figure's shirt. The cloth held for a moment, tore – or perhaps it was buttons giving way – then held again as Walsh's finger caught something stronger. He could hear help pounding towards him up the passage. The figure wrenched its arms clear of the hindering shirt and made a last valiant attempt to burst free, and indeed succeeded, but with Reg coming at full speed out of the passage that success was short-lived.

Walsh got to his feet and stared in amazement at what was still grasped in his hand. A torn black shirt and a bright red bra.

Sergeant Dodds stared with undisguised interest at the heaving bare breasts of the half-naked young girl whom Reg Finch was still gripping securely by the arms.

'You dirty bloody coppers,' the girl screeched between her gasps for breath. 'You wait till I tell the judge that you bastards ripped me clothes off and tried to rape me. Let me go. Let me go. You're hurting my arms.'

Sergeant Dodds licked his lips and grinned. 'You tried that line last time you were caught, Molly O'Brien, and it didn't get you anywhere then, and it won't do this time. You're a bloody fool, you are. You're on probation now, and if you waste the judge's time with silly stories like that, he'll put you inside Holloway, sure as eggs is eggs.'

The girl stopped struggling and her pinched pale face looked thoughtful. It seemed probable that tears were imminent.

Walsh held out the torn shirt, and the other garment. 'Let go of her, Reg,' he said quietly. 'Here, put these things back on, and make yourself decent.'

'Decent, he says?' She responded by giving a wriggle of her hips that set her flesh in motion again. 'And you lot staring so hard your tongues are hanging out. You'd like to get your hands on them, wouldn't you?' Her voice had turned coy and seductive. 'I can give each of you a real good time, if you promise to let me go. I won't tell nobody, honest.'

The arrival of a police patrol car interrupted that conversation.

# 3

There had been no overnight showers and daylight had come with a clear sky.

The sun's early rays brought only a suspicion of warmth, and the air was still invigoratingly cool and fresh. That coolness brought with it a heavy dew, which sheened the lawn an icy silver; crystal beaded a myriad of spiders' webs with tiny sparkling orbs.

Six men were at work, meticulously searching the flower beds and shrubs in Sir Gordon Lignum's back garden. Even with their shirt-sleeves rolled up most of them were nearly soaked already, with the water droplets that fell on them each time they touched a leaf or twig.

'So, Molly O'Brien was definitely round a neighbour's house with her mother during the period we think Lignum was killed,' Brenda mused thoughtfully. 'And neither of you took advantage of her offer of sexual delights? It's a good thing you two were there – I'm not so sure that Sergeant Dodds would have put duty before pleasure if he'd been on his own.'

Walsh looked at her, and frowned. From someone else that might have been sheer bitchiness, but coming from her, it was a relevant considered observation. Clearly Dodds had a weakness for the opposite sex, which was recognised by the females in the force. There had been no complaints made about the man as far as Walsh was aware, but if there was an element of risk with any officer, it ought to be looked into, and the man warned to watch his step; however, to take that sort of action more was needed than just Brenda's comment. This was a distraction he could well do without. Fortunately Reg came over and effectively diverted his mind.

'We'll search the gardens of these two houses on either side as well, boss,' Reg announced, 'just in case the weapon was thrown over the fence.'

Walsh nodded approvingly, but Brenda shook her head.

'You're wasting your time,' she said sceptically. 'The killer wouldn't have tossed the weapon where you could find it easily. If it's anywhere, it's deep in the river bottom. Those divers who are coming later won't find anything either. You'll have to dredge at least a couple of miles to even stand a chance.'

'You're a right little ray of sunshine this morning,' Reg muttered as he turned away, but there was no point in arguing over a statement that merely said that the chances of finding the murder weapon were small. They all knew that. However, the murder weapon, if it were found, might just provide some vital clue as to the killer's identity. So even if the chances of success were slim to the point of anorexia, a search had to be made. If it had to be done, it might just as well be done properly, and that was what Reg intended to do.


Lady Ingrid Lignum sat in a chair in the bright morning sunshine that bathed the paved garden terrace.

She was in her early thirties and nearly as tall as Walsh himself. Her fair hair hung in waves to her shoulders and an up-brushed fringe surmounted a rather square Scandinavian face that contained large eyes of faded cornflower blue. Her figure was solidly shapely too, firm and muscular, an ideal model for a Valkyrie Brünnhilde or perhaps an Iceni Boudicca, but this morning there was little regal or particularly imposing about her demeanour. She wore fawn linen slacks, sandals, and a red and white striped cotton blouse, but she slouched rather than reclined in the padded sun-chair, and her eyes were weary as they concentrated on the cup of coffee that she seemingly needed both hands to keep steady.

'Yes, I am ready for your questions,' she replied in a voice that was surprisingly soft and sweet, 'but my head to the rest of me is not quite joined on. I drank too much last night, I think.'

Walsh nodded understandingly. She certainly showed all the outward signs of someone suffering from a hangover. He would pose his questions gently to start with.

Brenda Phipps sat nearby, a writing pad on her lap, and she was watching Lady Lignum's face intently.

'It must have given you a tremendous shock, last night, coming home to find what you did,' Walsh said sympathetically.

'It certainly did. Poor Gordon. He was lying on the floor so still, and there was nothing I could do for him,' she replied, shaking her head regretfully. Her pale blue eyes blinked a few times as they looked directly at his face.

'I understand you were singing with the choral society last night.'

She shrugged her shoulders. 'It's not a real choral society, only a made-up one, and not very good. That is why we practised on a Saturday night, because the concert is in only two weeks. The male voices are very bad. The orchestra is good, they are young people from the schools, but the singing is not right, not yet. I think Beethoven's Ninth is too difficult without much practice,' she explained.

'Where were you rehearsing, and what time did it start?'

'At seven. It was at the school in Long Road. The one near the railway bridge.'

Out of the corner of his eye Walsh could see that Brenda was busy making notes. It would be necessary to check this story out thoroughly. Murder was too often a way of getting rid of an unwanted marriage partner.

'What time did you get home?' he asked. He knew the time of the 999 call, of course, but it was essential to try and account for every minute of her time yesterday evening.

Ingrid Lignum pursed her lips. 'It was before ten, I think, perhaps a quarter to. I put my car in the garage, and went in the front door. The lights were on in the house, of course. I called out to let Gordon know I was home, but there was no reply. That's why I went to look for him.'

'You went in the front door, not the side door then?'

'Yes. We usually keep the side gate bolted from the other side, but I don't know if it was so last night. It should have been.'

'And this french window to the patio, was that unlocked when you went off to your rehearsal?' Walsh asked.

Lady Lignum nodded.

'Did you see anyone hanging about near the front of the house? Any strange cars?'

This time she shook her head.

'Your husband was an archaeologist, I understand,' Walsh prompted.

'That is so. He's been attached to the University for several years, Professor Gladsbury's the principal. He can tell you more about Gordon's past than I can. He was one of the lecturers here when Gordon was a student.'

41

'Was your husband on his own when you left? Was he expecting visitors, do you know?'

'Gordon was on his own. I don't think he was expecting visitors. He never told me so, if he was,' she replied.

'What sort of person was he, your husband? Did he have any enemies?'

'Gordon was a very nice man, though often withdrawn into himself with his thoughts. Introverted is the right word, I think. He was teased much as a boy. I do not know why, but your schools can be cruel to one who is shy and quiet, can't they? He was a little innocent of life perhaps, and perhaps too proud of having a father with a title. Poor Gordon, perhaps he made enemies, but not violent ones. No, not violent ones.' She shook her head, setting her blonde hair waving. 'But lately his temper had been short. He had a tumour grow, here in his neck. It was very worrying, and I know he was frightened he would die, but he hated the thought of being talked about or people showing sympathy, so he told no one but me. It was not malignant though, his doctor told him the results of the tests only yesterday morning.' She wiped round an eye with her finger and let her head rest back, then she closed both eyes. 'We had a good life together, I think. I have many happy memories. We went to remote archaeological sites abroad, sometimes. Then we'd drive the Rover up into the mountains and sometimes we'd camp and sleep under the stars. There would be little villages with tiny happy children in ragged clothes and bare feet. The people at the sites were so friendly too. Here in Cambridge, we know many people. It was a good life for us, with parties and dinners and things, but I do not know what I will do – now I'm on my own.'

'Who will be the heir to your husband's title?' Walsh asked quietly.

She opened her eyes again. 'We have no children, so the tenth baronet will be a cousin, one of the family out in New Zealand. Adrian is his name. I have not met him.'

'Your husband had made a will, presumably?'

'Yes, I'm sure his affairs are well in good order. David Grant is his solicitor, and he can explain things better than I. The family fortune is in a trust, you see, and Gordon only had the interest, if he needed it. That will all pass to the cousin in New Zealand, but Gordon took out some pensions and insurance for me, in case anything happened to him. The trust owns this house, but I may still live here, unless I remarry, of course.'

Her eyes darkened fractionally as a wisp of cloud came before the sun. They were beautiful eyes, yet surprisingly cool and expressionless. Eyes could sometimes tell a great deal about what was going on in a person's mind, if you knew how to read them, and Walsh wasn't sure he understood these.

'Tell me about yourself, Lady Lignum. How did you meet Sir Gordon? You are Swedish, aren't you?'

A faint smile appeared on her lips as she paused to collect her thoughts.

'Yes, I am Swedish. My name is Ingrid Elsa Moulmark, and I was born in Vodalistat, which is a small town some two hundred kilometres north of Stockholm, thirty-odd years ago. My parents died when I was seven. I met Gordon about ten years ago, in Rome. I was studying art there. We became friends and he asked me to marry him. It was not difficult to say yes, you understand. So I came to live here in Cambridge with him. I have no family now in Sweden.'

'So you're an artist? I saw the sketch you made of your husband, the one in his study. I thought it was very good,' Walsh commented.

Ingrid smiled wanly. 'I teach at the Polytechnic two days a week, and one evening. Art and music are my interests, hobbies you might say, but I'm also involved with fund-raising for charities – children's charities. That is very important, don't you think?'

Walsh nodded. 'You say you don't know the combination of the safe in the study? Never mind, we'll get one of our chaps to open it. Thank you for talking to me. You'll finish that list of missing items as soon as you can, won't you? We'll leave you in peace, for now.'

'What did you make of her, Brenda?' Walsh asked when they'd met up with Reg Finch on the front drive. Brenda's opinions of her own sex were very valuable, with perceptive insights into character that were clear to her, yet only vague suspicions to a male, even one as experienced as himself.

'She's a hard nut, Chief, and as tough as old boots,' Brenda replied firmly.

Walsh looked at her in some surprise. 'There's more to her than meets the eye, is there?'

'I wouldn't be at all surprised.'

'A very attractive woman, I thought,' Reg Finch admitted.

'I doubt if you're the first to think so, Reg,' Brenda said implacably.

'I see,' Walsh muttered, then changed the subject. 'How has the search gone, Reg?'

Finch shook his head. 'No signs of the murder weapon, boss, or anything else. I've also been glancing through the house-to-house inquiry statements taken so far – no one round here saw anything suspicious or unusual.'

'Never mind, it's early days yet,' Walsh said philosophically. 'What I'd like you to do first thing tomorrow, Reg, is go and see this Professor Gladsbury at the Archaeological Unit and find out what he can tell us about Lignum. His wife said he was "attached" to the University, whatever that means. Brenda, you can take on this choral rehearsal. Have a chat with the conductor or whatever he's called. We'll need to check out Lady Lignum's alibi pretty thoroughly. I'll be seeing the C.C. first thing, and I've also got to get someone to open that safe. Maybe there'll be something in there to give us a lead.'

'Finished for the day?' Gwen Walsh asked when her husband walked into the kitchen.

'Hopefully so, unless anything else serious crops up,' Sidney replied as he filled the kettle and set about making coffee.

'You were up early. You didn't wake me when you went off, or last night when you came in,' Gwen commented.

'You were sleeping so soundly this morning that I didn't have the heart to disturb you. As for last night, well, I didn't need you, did I? Not when I'd spent most of the evening wrenching the bras off sexy eighteen-year-olds,' he responded with a wry smile, while watching her face for a reaction, but Gwen knew him too well, and there was none.

'You always were impatient with bras, Sidney. You never could get the hang of undoing the clip at the back with one hand,' she reminded him placidly.

'True, but this one had the clip at the front. They're much better. One quick tug, and they're off. It saves a lot of time.'

'At your age, you need the extra time. How many sexy eighteen-year-olds did you manage last night? One good one and I'd have thought you'd be a physical wreck for weeks.'

'This one must have been a bad one then – it's the third time she's been caught.'

'Caught? She tried to run away, did she? Shame on you for molesting a poor sweet innocent young –'

'Sweet and innocent? Molly O'Brien? You must be joking. It took three of us to nail her.'

'That's how you got your jeans in such a mess, was it? I've put them in the wash. Now, I'll fix you something to eat, if you like, and then would you give me a hand with the wallpapering upstairs, please? I tried to put a length up this afternoon, but I couldn't get it to go right. It kept bubbling up all over the place, and looked awful. I know you're tired, but I must get that room finished. The fitter's coming on Tuesday to lay the new carpet.' Gwen turned her head to look at him anxiously.

Walsh shrugged his shoulders reluctantly. This was the first he'd heard about a new carpet, and the idea of hanging wallpaper on a Sunday evening did not appeal to him at all. After he'd spoken to Lady Lignum that morning he'd been so busy, what with the autopsy to attend, house-to-house inquiry statements to read, and scene-of-crime photos to peruse, that he'd hardly found the time for even a cup of coffee. Now all he really wanted to do was to sit down quietly and let his mind relax, but he couldn't do that – if Gwen had problems with the wallpapering it wouldn't be for a want of trying, and she was obviously in a fix.

'No problem,' he said, smiling ruefully. 'It probably needs to soak for a while before it's hung. Never mind – you paste, I'll put it up.'

If they took it nice and steady they might get it finished before midnight, but at least that would be one job over and done with.


# 4


Detective Constable Brenda Phipps sat herself down on one of the rather tatty easy chairs in the school staff room.

'You were lucky to catch me in a free period, officer,' the tall, harassed-looking teacher said, pushing a pile of exercise books to one side of the table, then turning his chair so that he sat facing his visitor. 'What do you want to talk to me about?'

'One of the members of your choir,' Brenda Phipps stated bluntly.

'Which choir? This one here, St Paul's Church or the one for the combined schools concert?'

'The Beethoven's Ninth choir. Lady Lignum – one of the sopranos.'

'Oh yes, I know who you mean, of course. She's all right, she can sing, and speak German. I put her with the schoolgirls. They like her, and she helps them with their pronunciation. I need all the help I can get, I can tell you. They should have stuck to a straightforward orchestral piece. I said so at the time, but no, they would go ahead. The local choral societies had full programmes, and couldn't fit this in. They didn't want to, more likely. So I've had to organise an *ad hoc* choir out of schoolchildren, teachers and anyone else I can rope in. You need plenty of adult voices for that piece, children's voices are too sweet and thin, if you know what I mean. The orchestra's fine, very good, no problem there. Never mind, we'll manage.' He ran his hands through his hair in anguish and shrugged his shoulders at the same time. 'What's she been up to?'

'We're just trying to clarify her movements on Saturday evening. She says she was at a rehearsal from about seven until half-past nine. Could you confirm that?' Brenda asked.

The geography teacher-cum-choirmaster looked a little exasperated.

'There're over fifty people, you know. I had the male voices on their own for most of the time, they're my big problem. What the women did then I have no idea, probably they just stood around nattering. I had them all together for the last half-hour, and yes, Ingrid was there then, because I had a short chat with her afterwards.'

'You know her socially, do you?' Brenda asked, with eyebrows raised. He'd said the name 'Ingrid' with a strange softness, as though it were something precious, mystical even.

'Yes, I suppose I do, in a way. We've met several times at charity concerts. She's a very nice person, and attractive too.'

'Are you married?' Brenda inquired.

'I was. I'm not now. I'm a reconstituted bachelor, you might say.'


The entrance to the Archaeology building was unpretentious. The words cut into the limestone lintel over the arched entrance were the only indication of its existence down the narrow lane leading to the River Cam.

Reg Finch pushed open one of the solid wooden doors and stepped inside, moving out of a bright, sunny world into one which was dark and dankish.

Round the walls of the first room were rows of glass display cases, showing the development of stone tools from the sturdily crude palaeolithic, to the delicate microlithic and polished neolithic. Which was no mean feat in that confined space, but then, this was no museum for the general public; its displays of selected specimens were there purely for the benefit of student and scholar.

It was a collection that had started accumulating in those days when antiquarians – educated amateurs from Church and aristocracy – had no way of classifying or dating their finds, before the Carters, Wheelers and others of that ilk transformed an interesting hobby into the methodical discipline of the modern archaeologist.

Reg Finch wandered through the rooms looking for someone to guide him to the office and reception area, but without success. Finally he decided to take the initiative by going through a rear doorway marked 'Private'.

Down a bare carpetless corridor he found a room with an occupant.

He was a bespectacled young man of about twenty, with long lank dark hair pulled tight to the back of his neck in a pony tail.

'I'm looking for Professor Gladsbury. Can you help me, please?' Finch announced.

The young man sat at a table strewn with a number of different pieces of pottery, which he was obviously sorting into types.

'Old Gladsbury? We have something in common then; you're looking for the "Ancient One", and I'm trying to classify bits of his pottery.' He leaned back in his chair and sighed. 'We all seek to gain wisdom, but for many of us the door appears to be firmly locked. Still, we must persevere,' he went on despondently.

'Maybe so,' Reg Finch said with a slight smile, and reached forward to show his police warrant card, 'but I am a seeker after knowledge with a key that opens many doors. Now, would you direct me to, or take me to, your leader, please?'

The young man blinked, then took off his spectacles and rubbed at the bridge of his nose thoughtfully. His eyes were bright and clear, and very intelligent.

'That might not be easy. We haven't seen him here lately. It's his age probably; after all, he was old before anyone thought of inventing hills. He ought to retire, but when one gets a professorial chair as rich as his, you hang on to it as long as possible, and who can blame him? Is it him you really want, though? His Most High Eloquence, Sir Gordon Lignum, Bart, MA, BA, et cetera, or the cheerful chappie Charlie Choosely, MA, BA, et cetera, usually deal with things mundane when the Great Gladsbury's not about, which is most of the time.'

'The girl I spoke to on the phone earlier told me that the Great Gl . . . I mean Professor Gladsbury, would be here this morning, but I came in through the museum. I couldn't find another entrance.'

'That's round the corner, camouflaged to look like a common back door. It fools a lot of people, you included apparently. Right ho, most highly exalted visitor with the key that opens any door, I will guide you through this tortuous warren of a maze. It's risky though. Many of those who enter here get lost and lose their minds. They spend the rest of their lives wandering around muttering to themselves. We call them dons. When they finally croak it, we sell their bones to the medical labs for twenty pounds the set. Walk this way, please,' and the young man set off down the corridor with an excessively exaggerated limp, but only for two or three strides, then he walked perfectly normally.

Professor Gladsbury's room on the first floor was more like a disused storeroom than an office. He was a frail man with sparse white hair, and a mind that wandered.

Reg Finch found the task of sorting out the answers to his questions from wild lengthy ramblings both irksome and tedious. When he left, after about half an hour, he felt brainwashed and bewildered, having learned little of value about the life of the murdered Sir Gordon Lignum. However, a ten-minute chat with the young receptionist in the office downstairs was much more productive.


The Chief Constable's meeting had run on a little, so Detective Chief Inspector Sidney Walsh had to wait in the secretary's small annexed office.

'He won't be long, sir,' Madge said, smiling up from her word processor at one of her favourite senior officers. Walsh was always polite and pleasant, with none of the dirty jokes and innuendoes that she had to put up with from some.

'It sounds as though they're finishing now,' she announced a few moments later, her head cocked to one side like a cheeky sparrow. 'Give him another minute. He'll go to his private loo next. He's as regular as clockwork, you know. When I hear it flush I'll take in his coffee, and tell him you're here.'

Walsh smiled and nodded.

When the C.C. wasn't away at some conference or other, he always had a full day. Mostly liaising with his departmental heads about the thousand and one things needed to manage the diverse activities of an active police force. Walsh, as head of the serious crime team, was one of a few executives who could obtain almost immediate access.

The tall, burly, red-faced C.C. was standing by the window, coffee cup in hand, when Walsh walked in.

'Help yourself,' he said, waving a hand in the direction of the coffee pot on his large oak desk. 'A baronet this time, I gather, bashed on the head with an iron bar.'

'That's right. Sir Gordon Lignum, archaeologist and the ninth holder of the title. He lived in a nice house in Newnham that backs on to the river, with a Swedish wife ten years or so younger than himself. There were no children,' Walsh replied as he poured himself a coffee.

'Packstone tells me that whoever did it took anything of value that was light and easy to carry. Do you reckon it was a sneak thief nutter who bonked Lignum on the head to keep him quiet, but bonked a bit too hard?'

Walsh shrugged. 'It's possible. We caught one break-in specialist last night, Molly O'Brien, but her mother and a neighbour have given her an alibi that won't be easy to break. The only thing I don't like about the robbery idea is that Lignum appears to have been working in his study while listening to some music. You'd have thought a good sneak thief could have got in and out without disturbing him.'

50

'I can't see the O'Brien girl going in for violence, but you never know,' the C.C. commented.

'There was a small old-fashioned safe in the study that the robber obviously couldn't open. Inside were some family papers, but there was also a thousand pounds in ten-pound notes, still in the bank's original wrappers. I'm interested in that money because Lignum banked with a Cambridge branch, and that lot came from London,' Walsh explained, putting his empty coffee cup down on the desk.

'What about Lignum's widow? Packstone said she was an attractive long-legged blonde?'

'She was out rehearsing with a choir. Something to do with a Beethoven's Ninth concert. We're checking her story, of course.'

'Beethoven's Ninth? The combined schools orchestra? My wife wants me to flog some of the tickets for that. She's a governor of one of the schools, you know. The proceeds go to some charity or other. I'll tell her to put you down for a couple, Sidney. No, I'd better make that four. You can have a word with Finch and young Phipps and get them to go too. That'll help get rid of some of the blasted things. Anything else to tell me?'

'Not a lot. Lignum was writing an archaeological report when he was killed. The top sheet was missing, but he'd been doodling on it. He'd written "B9" and "K9" and underlined them. That might be important.'

' "B9" sounds like Beethoven's Ninth,' the C.C. suggested.

'Could be, but Lignum was also the ninth baronet. I don't know what they mean yet. Anyway, I want to ask the Swedish police to check out his wife's background, and there's the new heir to the title, too. He's a New Zealander, living in Wellington. If he was at home that night we don't need to worry about him, of course. I've drafted out these official requests for your signature.'

The C.C. glanced at them, then pressed a button on his intercom console, summoning his secretary.

'Get these typed up straight away, Madge. I want them faxed off as soon as possible.'

'Yes, sir,' Madge said. On the way out she turned to Walsh. 'Professor Hughes of Downing College has been on the phone for you, Inspector. He'd like to have a word with you when you're free.'

'What's old Hughes want, Sidney?' the C.C. demanded.

Walsh shook his head. 'I've no idea.'

'All right then. Now, you say that Lignum had used an ultra-violet marker to write his postcode on most of the items that were stolen. It'd be mighty handy if they turned up in an antique shop somewhere, wouldn't it? What have you done about them?'

'Nothing yet. When Lady Lignum's finished the list, I'll have it circulated nationwide.'

Professor Edwin Hughes was a short, elderly, nearly bald-headed man of rotund stature. He wore neat white linen trousers and a tartan shirt of such bright vivid colours that had its design been of a real clan, then the people of Scotland would never have achieved a reputation for being a dour race.

Normally he was a cheerful jaunty man, but this afternoon, as he welcomed Detective Chief Inspector Walsh into his comfortably furnished Downing College rooms, he looked concerned and not a little worried.

Nevertheless, he politely ushered his guest to a leather-upholstered, high-backed wing chair, near one of the leaded mullioned windows that overlooked the cobbled courtyard below.

Before sitting down Walsh had a quick look round the room. There were some new paintings hanging on these walls that he would like the chance to peruse. Some of Downing College's varied art collection found its way on to the walls of the dons' apartments, and Walsh had found great pleasure in studying them in the past. In fact, they had been the reason for him setting up an easel in the spare small bedroom and trying his hand with paints and a brush. Firstly watercolours, but more recently with oils.

'It's good of you to come over so promptly, but it's difficult to know just where to start, Inspector,' Hughes said hesitantly. 'I suppose I want to make a request – ask a favour of you.'

Walsh pursed his lips. Favours asked of a police officer usually meant the turning of a blind eye to some transgression of the law, or even interference with some legal process, and much as he liked and respected this old professor, who had indeed been very helpful in some past investigations, there was no way that he would do either of those things. Some evidence of these thoughts must have shown on his face, for Hughes shook his head vigorously.

'Oh no. I'm not about to ask you to bend the law. It's more of a request for you to extend your investigations to include something that might well be related to them anyway, but naturally, I am making certain assumptions.'

'Why not start at the beginning?' Walsh said, smiling at his host's unaccustomed confusion.

'That is the best way,' Hughes agreed. 'Firstly, though, please clarify one thing for me. It has been announced on the local radio that Sir Gordon Lignum was found dead on Saturday night, in suspicious circumstances. Are you investigating his death?'

'I am,' Walsh replied shortly.

'Good. You know, of course, that Sir Gordon was an archaeologist; perhaps you also know that he was in charge of an excavation out at Hinching Park, near Huntingdon. No? You haven't got that far yet. Well, let me tell you what I know about it. It's a site where the developer is required by the terms of the planning consent to sponsor and finance an archaeological survey, and any subsequent excavations, if that survey finds anything of historical interest,' Hughes explained.

Then he went on to tell the story of the finding of the fragment of clay tablet by the young excavator, Melissa Fairbrother, and of the resultant altercation, when Sir Gordon Lignum had accused the young Scot, Andrew MacGregor, of having deliberately planted the tablet there.

'Sir Gordon', Hughes continued, 'apparently acted rather out of character by losing his temper, and he threatened to have both youngsters sent down from the University. Now, that's a very serious matter, you understand. Being sent down, even for a short period, can have a devastating effect on the student and his future career. It does not reflect well upon his college either, so it's not a matter to be treated lightly.'

'You're surely not suggesting that a mere practical joke warrants police investigation, professor?' Walsh interrupted.

Hughes held up a hand. 'Hear me out, please. I have not finished setting out this unfortunate scenario. It appears that these two youngsters spent much of Saturday evening punting on the upper Cam, and Sir Gordon's house backs on to the river, doesn't it? As soon as they realised how near they'd been to the scene of the crime, they came to see me. They thought it was better to tell their story openly, even if it might put them on your suspect list,' the professor explained.

'Quite right! As a motive the sending-down threat sounds a bit thin, but if they were on that part of the river at the time we believe Lignum was killed, then yes, we are going to be interested in them. Did they mention whether one of my officers had already interviewed them?'

Hughes nodded. 'Their punt was in fact requisitioned by one of your lady officers. From their description it rather sounds as if it might have been young Brenda. Apparently she slipped and got soaked when she tried to get aboard the punt. These young people are inclined to be a little headstrong at times, aren't they? However, the nature of the crime committed that night was not stated, and neither student knew then that Sir Gordon lived on that stretch of river. They've asked my help and advice. That's why I'm talking to you now.' Hughes raised his eyebrows and waited for Walsh's reaction.

'Interesting!' Walsh commented cautiously. 'It's a bit of a coincidence, those two being on the river at that particular time, isn't it?'

'On the face of it, it might appear so, but young MacGregor has been earning extra cash to eke out his grant by working weekends and evenings for a boat hire firm. It's a perk of the job, apparently, that he can have free use of a boat after hours, and he takes full advantage of it. Sometimes on his own, but lately in the company of this Fairbrother girl. What I find surprising, though, is Lignum's reaction to this practical joke business,' Hughes admitted. His agitation had eased apparently, for he now sat himself down. 'He's worked with students for years. You'd have thought he could handle their high spirits.'

'His wife said that he'd developed a tumour in his neck, and he only learned it was not malignant on the day that he died,' Walsh explained.

Hughes nodded understandingly. 'I wasn't aware of that. I didn't know him very well. Yes, that could easily have made him short-tempered. Generally we older folk cope reasonably well with the undergraduates' lively sense of humour. They are all intelligent young people of course, or they wouldn't be here, but they are away from home, some of them for the first time. It's part of our job to help them develop their personalities, but in the process of maturing they do sometimes show extremes of behaviour, even stupidity. Then we need tolerance and understanding.'

'Planting a cuneiform tablet on an archaeological site comes under the stupid category, does it?' Walsh asked. 'How did they get hold of it in the first place? I'd have thought such things were not easy to come by. Are they?'

Hughes looked bemused for a moment. 'No, I don't suppose they are, but it was a stupid thing to do, certainly. Consider the effect if it had been taken seriously, and been publicised. A tablet written in cuneiform being found on a rather bland inconsequential site in Huntingdonshire? It would have caused much scorn and no little ribaldry among the archaeological fraternity. They're not a discipline noted for their tolerance of anything which doesn't conform to accepted views,' Hughes explained.

Walsh resisted the temptation to yawn. 'What's so special about a cuneiform tablet being discovered in England?' he asked, then wished he hadn't.

Hughes blinked more in shock than surprise. 'There's none ever been found in Northern Europe before,' he explained with undisguised patience. 'Cuneiform writing was developed by the Sumerians, you know. It was impressed on to soft clay using a narrow piece of reed or wood, and the clay was baked hard later, to make it permanent. Once such writing had become established, it spread throughout the Middle East, and was adopted by other empires to write other languages, even though by then the Sumerians had almost faded out of history. The Babylonians, the Akkadians, the Hittites, even the Egyptians used it, but, as I say, it never spread into Northern Europe.'

The word Hittite rang a bell, and Walsh hastily set his mind to recalling the wording on the print of the ancient ruined city that had hung on the wall in Sir Gordon Lignum's study.

'So, the finding in Huntingdonshire of a clay tablet dated, presumably, *circa* 1300 BC, and originating from the Hittite capital, Hattusa, in Turkey, would be ridiculed by the archaeological world, would it? Was it small or large, this tablet?'

Hughes now seemed surprised at the extent of Walsh's historical knowledge.

'It was about the size of a round of bread, apparently, but we don't know what language it was, because Sir Gordon took it away with him. What he did with it we don't know. Hopefully you'll find it somewhere in his house. The girl, Fairbrother, took some photographs while it was still embedded in the ground, but then she went and lost her camera, so that's no help.'

'We've found nothing like that so far as I know, but I'll have a search made for it, certainly. You say MacGregor and Fairbrother deny planting the tablet. If they're telling the truth, then either someone else put it there, or the find, in spite of what you say, is actually genuine.'

Hughes pulled a long face. 'The latter would be unique, unexpected and very unlikely. I suppose you could pose the possibility that there had been some sort of trading connections between this country and the Middle Eastern civilisations of those times. After all, in the Roman period people travelled all over the continent, so you could ask why it should have been significantly different two thousand years earlier.' Hughes waved a plump hand as though to emphasise the point. 'However, supporting historical evidence is non-existent. Mind you, Irish mythology does refer to the land of Dana, or Diana, which you could postulate was at that end of the Mediterranean, and a tribe known as the Chatti or Hatti did arrive in Saxony about 300 BC; they might have been the remnants of the Hattusa-based Hittite empire. Still, although such doubtful evidence might satisfy believers in flying saucers, it won't do for hidebound academics. Me? I'd love to see the accepted ideas of the historians' world turned upside down. If this Huntingdon tablet were genuine, it would certainly be one of the most important finds made in this country recently. The site would need to be intensively excavated to look for any supporting evidence, and that could take a long time.' Hughes grinned broadly. 'The developers wouldn't be happy with that, would they? It could cost them a fortune. Look what happened when they unearthed the foundations of that Shakespeare theatre in London.'

'I can't afford to be romantic in my line of business,' Walsh admitted cautiously. 'I'm supposed to deal only with facts, but sometimes it's difficult to know when a fact is a fact. Lignum threatened these two students with expulsion. What action did he subsequently take?'

'None that I know of. Perhaps it was being held in abeyance until the head of the department, Professor Gladsbury, got back to Cambridge. Choosely might know. He's Gladsbury's other assistant.'

'Was the tablet found at a depth or in a stratum in keeping with its real age?' Walsh asked.

'I don't know,' Hughes admitted.

'Never mind, you've given me a lot to think about as it is,' Walsh said. 'From what you've told me, this cuneiform tablet business does appear to be relevant to our inquiries. We'll interview Fairbrother and MacGregor tomorrow, and as for the archaeological aspect, I'll put Reg Finch on to that – he might even get Forensic involved if he thinks they can help.'

Hughes smiled brightly. 'Thank you, Inspector. I was hoping you'd say that. It effectively makes this sending-down matter *sub judice*. Maybe in time the whole distasteful incident can be resolved without affecting the good name of the college.'

'As far as this tablet business is concerned, with the principal piece of evidence and the principal witness both conveniently lost or out of the way, I really don't see how your college authorities could proceed anyway. Of course, that might be just what Sir Gordon Lignum's killer had in mind,' Walsh observed drily.

He had the dubious pleasure of seeing Hughes's cheerful smile change quickly back to an expression of serious thoughtfulness.


David Grant, the solicitor, was a tall, fit-looking man, probably in his forties. His face was tanned and ruggedly handsome as he leaned forward, his elbows on his desk.

'This is all most distressing, Chief Inspector. I've always considered Gordon and Ingrid as friends of mine, not just clients, so it's difficult to talk dispassionately about them, after such a tragedy.'

'You've known them for some time then?' Walsh asked.

'I acted for Gordon on a few small matters here in Cambridge while his father was still alive. Then, when one of the trustees wanted to retire, Gordon recommended my appointment in his place.'

'Tell me about the trust,' Walsh prompted.

'It's nothing complicated. The seventh baronet had horrendous death duties when the sixth died, and he had to sell the family estate in Berkshire to raise the money. So he put whatever was left, plus what he'd accumulated later from his business deals, into a trust, to ensure that a similar situation never arose again. Now, each new baronet effectively becomes a working fund manager, and is entitled to draw a salary equal to the trust's net income – with some restrictions. For instance, if the overall capital value of the trust's assets should go down for any reason, then a percentage of the income has to be reinvested, until the shortfall has been made up,' Grant explained.

'His house in Newnham is owned by the trust, I understand.'

'Yes. That's a provision in the trust, so that the title holder can be provided with a suitable residence. Such places are normally a good investment anyway. Naturally the widow is entitled to live there until she dies, or remarries.'

'So Lignum was a very wealthy man, from an income point of view?' Walsh suggested.

Grant shook his head. 'I wouldn't say so. He had his salary from the Archaeological Foundation, of course, but the trust . . . how can I put it? Well, it's been going through a rather lean time because of this recession. We've had to write down the values of some of our property investments, and we lost a large sum in the BCCI collapse. So during the past few years much of the income has had to be reinvested, leaving relatively little for Gordon to draw on. Not that he cared, his interests in life were archaeology, and Ingrid, of course.'

'She benefits from pension funds and insurances, I understand,' Walsh stated.

'That's so. As I explained to her yesterday evening, she should be comfortably provided for, which is what we, that is, Gordon wanted. She was quite devastated, poor thing.'

Grant's concern for his dead client's wife was obviously genuine, but there was also just the hint that he saw himself as her guide and protector. A little verbal prod might bring out his feelings more clearly.

'So she rang you at home, did she? Wanting to know how she stood financially, I suppose, or did she just want some company?'

'Not at all,' Grant replied indignantly. 'She's a very nice person, and was utterly devoted to Gordon. I'm sure that at the moment money is the last thing she's thinking about. She just thought that someone ought to inform Gordon's cousin in New Zealand. Naturally, I went round to see her straight away – at least I could be supportive and understanding, as a friend should.'

'Are you married, Mr Grant?' Walsh asked thoughtfully.

'Me? No! I've never met the right woman, I suppose.'

'I see,' Walsh mused. 'Getting back to this trust, how much is it worth at the present moment?'

'At the last full valuation, including the house in Newnham, just over a million pounds. That's only marginally more than when Gordon's father died, so, bearing in mind inflation over the past seven years, we trustees haven't done very well, have we?'

Walsh shrugged his shoulders non-committally. 'Sir Gordon's financial affairs might possibly have some bearing on our investigations, so I'd like copies of the trust's accounts, and its transactions over the last seven years, for our files, if you'd be so kind, and also a copy of his will. Where were you on Saturday evening, by the way?'

'Good Lord, you don't suppose I killed Gordon, do you?'

'It's just a routine question. Where were you?'

'At the golf club, as a matter of fact all evening.'


'So the company developing this site at Hinching Park would have to delay starting work, and meet the costs of a long excavation, Chief. They'd be delighted if this tablet business was brushed under the carpet as a practical joke,' Brenda observed from where she stood gazing out of the window of Walsh's office on the second floor of police headquarters.

'If this MacGregor killed Lignum then Fairbrother must be his accomplice, boss,' Reg Finch suggested. 'She'd be the weak link. It oughtn't to be difficult to make her crack up and spill the beans.'

60

'Well, you've done well for suspects, Chief. Two undergraduates, the site developers, and a solicitor who's obviously under Lady Ingrid Lignum's attractive spell. So you did better than either of us,' Brenda went on. 'I've been dashing around the town talking to members of this Beethoven's Ninth choir, and I still can't say positively that Lady Lignum stayed at that rehearsal all the time. I'm not even sure that the choirmaster was telling the truth when he said she was there at the end – he went a bit pink round the gills when her name was mentioned, so there might just be some sort of relationship between the two of them. Anyway, while the male singers were rehearsing on their own the women milled around outside chatting for well over half an hour, and that's really the period I can't pin down. It's quite long enough for her to have gone home, bashed her old man on the head and got back to the rehearsal. Still, I've more to interview yet, so maybe one of those will support her alibi.'

'My interview with Professor Gladsbury was soul-destroying,' Reg Finch admitted. 'The old boy's mind kept wandering so much that I'm not really sure if he understood quite why I was there. I ended up learning more about Sir Gordon by talking to Gladsbury's secretary. Apparently the foundation that funds that particular professorship is very generous, as well as being prestigious. Gladsbury's job is considered a real plum in the archaeological world, which is why he doesn't want to retire. Lignum, as his senior assistant, had already been appointed to succeed him when he did go. Now Charlie Choosely stands a good chance of taking over. He'll be lucky if he does. The funding for archaeology has been cut dramatically over the last few years, and although they might not actually be on the dole, there's quite a few archaeologists having to scratch around to make ends meet.'

'I thought that's what they did anyway – scratch around,' Brenda added humorously. 'So, getting Lignum out of the way could benefit this Choosely fellow. He ought to go on the list, too.'

'Where was Choosely last night, Reg?' Walsh asked.

'I don't know, I haven't met him yet.'

'It's a bit late this evening, but see him in the morning, and tell him we're going to need a thorough investigation of the area in which this wretched cuneiform tablet was found. I'll have a word with Packstone and see if I can get Forensic involved. It might lead to the most scientific archaeological excavation ever done in this part of the world,' Walsh suggested.

Reg looked sceptical. 'I doubt whether our fellows have ever used carbon 14 dating in an investigation. Still, it could prove interesting.'

'I'm sure Packstone can handle it, Reg. Right, then there's MacGregor and Fairbrother to see first thing in the morning as well. We'll do that, Brenda, you and me. Any other questions? No? Good. Now just one last thing. The C.C.'s palmed some tickets for this Beethoven's Ninth concert on to us. His wife's a school governor, you see, but they don't come any cheaper because of that. Gwen's bound to want to go, and you're a Beethoven fan too, aren't you, Brenda? What about you, Reg?'

Reg looked thoughtful for a moment, then nodded. 'We'll have four tickets, boss. Margaret and me, we'll take young Julie and her friend from the orphanage. They'll like that, I think.'


'There's a rather unusual problem come up on this Lignum case, Richard,' Walsh said to Packstone in the office of the forensic department. 'I'm in need of your expert advice and guidance.'

Packstone's eyes brightened up with interest, and he leaned forward on his desk with chin in hand and eyebrows raised. Much of the work in the forensic section consisted of mechanical and methodical procedures of scientific analysis. It required much dedicated concentration, but rarely nowadays did it throw up a really testing mental challenge. There was in Packstone's mental make-up a yearning to be challenged by problems, and he appeased that yearning to some extent with his hobby of cryptology.

'Ask away,' he replied with undisguised eagerness.

Walsh explained the circumstances surrounding the finding of the fragment of cuneiform tablet at the site near Huntingdon, and the resultant angry outburst from Sir Gordon Lignum.

'This fragment of a tablet is now missing, you say? Mind you, it wouldn't matter whether the language was Hittite, Babylonian or Sumerian. Anyone who proposed the find as genuine would be in for a rough ride,' Packstone observed thoughtfully. 'How do you think I might be able to help?'

'That part of the site where the tablet was found has been sealed off. I was wondering if you, or one of your chaps, would go out there with Reg Finch and check out the spot where the tablet was found. Take soil samples or something. I know that from the historical point of view the find is all wrong, but before I spend too much time worrying about who might have planted it, I would like to be absolutely certain that it was planted,' Walsh said, while idly rapping his fingers on the desk.

'We can test for uniform compaction in the soil beneath and round about where it was found. That would tell us whether the ground had been disturbed, and we can possibly find something to date the layer. I'll tell you what I'll do, Sidney. I'll go with Reg myself. Get him to fix up a time, and let me know.'

'Thanks. Now I know it's a bit early yet,' Walsh said hopefully, 'but have you found anything useful at Lignum's house?'

Packstone grimaced. There was a lot to do before he would be prepared to give a full report, and he never liked to commit himself beforehand, yet he quite understood an investigating officer's need to know quickly anything that might help the inquiry, particularly in the early stages.

'It depends what you mean by useful,' he muttered cautiously. 'There isn't an awful lot to go on. We do have traces of body debris from the carpets. Hairs, flakes of dead skin and so on. Those, of course, are being compared with the bona fide occupants of the house. In time, by elimination, we might come up with some from a stranger.'

Walsh looked gloomy. 'I suppose it's the same with fingerprints?'

Packstone nodded; his long fingers twisted a paperclip out of shape, then used one end to clean his left thumbnail. 'The last person to touch the outer door handle of the study wore gloves – well-used leather gloves. We found the same sort of smudges on the french window handle and two of the bedroom doors. Other than that, we spent a lot of time studying the surfaces of the carpets in the house, and what I can tell you is that someone who had been in that room recently had faint traces of oil on one of their shoes. It wasn't Lignum, or his wife, I've checked them.'

'Oil? The intruder might have stepped in some oil? What kind of oil?' Walsh asked.

'The nearest spectrographic match we can find is of a gearbox oil, but we'll be doing a detailed chemical analysis to try and confirm that. I'll let you know for certain later.'

'Gearbox oil? Car or motor bike?' Walsh asked.

Packstone shook his head. 'It would be a high-revving engine, probably a motor bike, but you'd better wait until the confirmatory analysis is completed before you start jumping to conclusions.'

# 5

It was a lean, elderly, grey-haired woman who opened the door of the tall Victorian terraced house. Her keen blue eyes looked suspiciously at the two police officers standing on the front step.

'We've come to see Miss Melissa Fairbrother. She is expecting us,' Walsh announced with a friendly smile.

'Oh, ah. You're the people come to see her about a holiday job in a museum, are you? Seems funny to me, interviewing a young girl in her bed-sit,' the woman announced suspiciously, clearly unaffected by Walsh's charm.

'We like to talk to them where they can feel relaxed,' Walsh replied, still maintaining his smile, but now a trifle woodenly. Clearly Melissa Fairbrother had considered that a visit by the police in their official capacity might cause complications in her life-style, and had invented another, somewhat implausible reason to account for their presence. He was quite happy to play along with that.

'You're her landlady, are you? What's she like? Keeps her room tidy, does she? Sober habits? Gets on well with your other guests? That sort of thing?'

'Course she does. She wouldn't have stayed here long if she didn't. I won't have no trouble-makers here in my place, whatever country they come from. Not that I'm strict, mind you, but you've got to have rules, haven't you?' She stepped back rather reluctantly into the hallway, to make room for her visitors to enter.

'You have girls from many different countries, do you?' Brenda Phipps asked. 'That must be very interesting.'

'I has them from all over the place. Japan, America, Australia. Black ones, yellow ones, brown ones, it don't bother me, as long as they're clean, decent and can get on with each other. Learning languages, a lot of them, but this Fairbrother's a brainy one, she's at this newfangled Churchill College. Her room's on the first landing – number 4. You can see yourselves up.'


'Yes, I'm Melissa Fairbrother. Do come in. I hope you don't mind being prospective employers, but my landlady's a bit of a stickler. If she knew you were police, my name would be mud. Oh! Hello, Chief Constable Brenda. I didn't recognise you at first. You're none the worse from your dip in the river the other night, I trust,' the dark-skinned girl said as she held the door open wide.

'I'm fine, thanks,' Brenda responded, looking quickly round the room. It was small, yet seemed to contain all the essentials. A narrow divan bed now had cheerfully coloured cushions leaning against the wall to make it into a tolerable daytime settee, and bookcases and cupboards gave some storage space. It was adequate, provided the occupant was tidy with her belongings, yet Brenda had seen prison cells with more space, and better furnishings.

'This is my Big White Chief, Melissa, Detective Chief Inspector Walsh,' she went on.

'I'm pleased to meet you,' Walsh uttered conventionally, his smile now seemingly fixed permanently. Melissa Fairbrother was an attractive young woman. She had high cheekbones, a narrow, slightly hooked nose and large dark eyes that just now looked a little tired or were they expressing worry and concern? It was difficult to be sure. She wore mauve jeans and a woollen sweater made up of many colours, and she was probably of Ethiopian or Somalian ancestry, Walsh thought, although English was clearly her native tongue.

'Let's start off with this cuneiform tablet,' Walsh suggested when they'd sat down. 'You were working on your own in the trench when you found it, I believe. Tell us what happened.'

'There's not much to tell, really,' Melissa replied. 'I was working in trench "K". That's just a straightforward trench being cut right across the site; it'll be dug down to the bed-rock – or, in this case, boulder-clay. It exposes all the different layers, you see, like the side of a steep cliff. The layers can then be dated, to provide reference points for finds made in the other parts of the site. Anyway, I'd come across some dark carboniferous material the day before. You know, charcoal, burnt wood, the sort of thing that might accumulate over the years on a fireplace, or it could have been a funeral pyre, or even just a tree struck by lightning. I'd cleared a lot of it, and the tablet appeared just beneath.' She shook her head uncertainly. 'I still can't see how that soil could have been disturbed overnight. I'm sure I would have noticed the changes in colour and texture. We're looking out for that kind of thing all the time, you see – a soil stain may be all that's left of a bone or piece of iron.'

'What was it like, this tablet?' Brenda asked, her eyes still watching the other's face keenly.

'In size? About four inches by six. At first it seemed a darkish white in colour. I thought then that it might be a piece of bone, but as I cleared more, it came up a pinkish red. By then, of course, I could see the cuneiform impressions on it.'

'Did you actually lift it clear of the ground?' Walsh wanted to know.

Again Melissa shook her head. 'I'd cleared most of it before I called Tiny over. He cleared a bit more, then fetched Sir Gordon. That's when things got a bit silly. Sir Gordon lost his temper and took the tablet away, before the official photos could be taken.' The memory of those events seemed to be distressing, for the girl's fingers started twisting themselves together nervously.

'You took some photos yourself, I understand,' Walsh prompted.

'That's right, I did, but what happened to my camera afterwards I don't know. I was a bit upset at the time, you understand. I thought I'd put it in my duffle bag with the rest of my bits and pieces, but when I came to look for it later, I couldn't find it.'

'Let's move on to last Saturday evening. Did you stop anywhere on your way upriver, and did either of you get off the punt?' Brenda asked.

'We went straight up to Byron's Pool, in Grantchester –' Melissa stopped abruptly because the door suddenly burst open, and a girl strode in.

This girl had obviously just had a bath, for one damp towel hung over her arm, and another was wrapped turban-like round her wet hair, but other than that strange headgear, she was completely naked. She was slender, skinny even, but otherwise well formed. A white-skinned young woman with large flashing dark eyes set deep under heavy black eyebrows.

'Mel –' she said, then stopped short as she realised there were visitors present, and one of them a male.

'Whoops! Sorry!' she exclaimed, hastily draping the loose towel over the front of her body. 'Mel, lend me your hair drier, will you? Some thieving swagger's had mine away,' she went on, apparently quite unconcerned by her immodest entry.

Melissa frowned, but reached up to take a drier from a shelf. 'All right, but don't lose it, Judy. It's the second one I've had to buy this term.'

'Don't worry. I'll give it you back,' the girl Judy said, and as she turned to go out of the door she flashed a broad smile at Walsh, who had been watching these events with a keen professional interest.

'Sorry about that,' Melissa apologised, seemingly glad of the interruption to the questioning, and in no great hurry to let it recommence, 'but entertaining males here in these rooms is absolutely forbidden. Well, only parents, or like you, on business. Decorum tends to go by the board. Mind you, some of the girls here have no modesty anyway. That girl, Judy, hasn't been here long. She's an Australian doing languages at one of the schools, though she seems to spend most of her time drawing. She did that sketch of me that's hanging on the wall over there. It's good isn't it? It only took her a few minutes.'

'It's excellent, I'd say,' Walsh declared enviously. His own efforts at painting were made more difficult by his lack of expertise in simple line drawing. This sketch of Melissa was so well done that her face seemed alive and even to stand out from the paper.

'Tell us a little about yourself, Melissa,' he went on to ask. 'Where you come from, what your parents do, what your plans for the future are?'

'My parents live in Northampton. Dad's a doctor, a GP. My mother's a schoolteacher. As for my future, I don't know what that will be now. I had planned to get my degree in history first and then see what was available, but that all seems hazy at the moment.'

'I see. Now this man you call Tiny, Andrew MacGregor, he's a bit of a practical joker, I understand. How well do you know him?'

Melissa frowned. 'I wouldn't say that he was a practical joker. Not as I understand one, anyway. He's no stupid itching powder, whoopee cushion type. Sure, he's got a sense of humour and can see the funny side of things, but that's as far as it goes. He's a Scot of course, and really he's a bit shy. I like him. I've known him for about a year, but it's only this last week or two we've spent a lot of time together. We're not lovers, if that's what you think. I don't think he's the sleep-about kind, and neither am I. We're just good friends, very good friends.' Melissa's bottom lip started to flutter and she used a finger to wipe at an eye. 'Sir Gordon had no reason to fly off the handle at Tiny and me like he did. I know you say that he thought he'd got cancer, and in the normal way I'd feel sorry, but even so it was very wrong of him. It's been horrible for Tiny and for me being accused of something we didn't do, and now we're suspected of killing him too. No, I haven't got a motor bike.'

Then Melissa's youthful resilience gave way, and she started sobbing into a handkerchief.


'Is there anything in the post for me this morning, Madge?' the Chief Constable asked his secretary as he poured himself a second cup of coffee.

It was rather a silly question, since by the C.C.'s own decree all letters sent to the Constabulary were required to be addressed to the Chief Constable. If any were not, it didn't matter; his staff would still open them and sort them into the different departments, for him to peruse before they were finally distributed. That was one way the C.C. had of ensuring he knew what was going on in his organisation. What his question to Madge really meant was, were there any incoming letters that only he could deal with?

'Nothing of importance, but there is a rather amusing letter, a well-written one, from a woman with a broken leg in Addenbrooke's Hospital. She says the nursing staff are treating her well,' Madge said as she laid the bulky correspondence file on the C.C.'s broad oak desk.

'What the devil's that got to do with me?'

'She says you'd say that.'

The C.C. looked round, his bushy eyebrows raised in surprise. Then he glanced down at his watch.

'Oh she does, does she? Well, read it out then, if it's not too long.'

'She says she was knocked off her motor bike by a car that pulled straight out in front of her without warning, and nearly a whole week has passed, and still no police officer has been to see her to take her statement. She assumes a statement will be needed before we can charge the driver with dangerous driving, or driving without due care. She doesn't mind which, so long as he is prosecuted.'

'She's being a bit vindictive isn't she? Still, someone should have been out to see her by now,' the C.C. muttered as he stared out of the window.

'She says you might say that too. She goes on, ". . . as I have a compound fracture of my left leg and a dislocated hip, and face the possibility of a lifetime limp, as well as being confined to this bed for the next three months, you might well think I have cause to be vindictive." '

'Fair comment. I wouldn't be too pleased if it happened to me.'

'She then goes on to say that someone caught speeding, even in a safe car on a safe road, will inevitably be punished. "How much more so should someone who, through sheer negligence or incompetence, puts at risk not only his own life, but those of others." '

'Very true.'

' "Not long ago," she writes, "the government ran a series of adverts on TV, warning car drivers to watch out for motor cycles, but the fact is that only when the mindless legions of drivers who say, "Sorry, I didn't see you," know for certain that their punishment will be imprisonment or, better still, the firing squad, will they take the trouble to look properly before pulling out. That should apply, whoever the driver is." '

'I couldn't agree with her more, except about the firing squad. That's going a bit too far, but it's not our fault, we can only apply the law as it stands. It's the government and the courts that fix the punishment,' the C.C. commented.

70

'She ends up by saying, "I do hope that knights of the realm like Sir Gordon Lignum have no greater privileges than the rest of the population." She signs her letter "Samantha Leverington, Mrs".'

'Who? What was that name?' the C.C. barked out suddenly, as he swung round from the window to face her.

'Mrs Samantha Leverington.'

'Not that one. The "Sir" someone or other.'

'Sir Gordon Lignum.'

The C.C. rubbed his chin thoughtfully. 'He was a baronet, not a knight of the realm. Never mind, do a photocopy of that letter, Madge,' he instructed, 'and then get on to the appropriate Traffic area for the details of that woman's accident. See that Sidney Walsh has them as soon as you can. Sir Gordon was obviously one of the "I didn't see you" brigade. He won't lose his driving licence or get prosecuted, however bad the injuries he may have caused. That's a privilege all murdered men have, I suppose.'

Andrew MacGregor politely offered to make coffee for his visitors.

'Thank you, no,' Walsh said as he sat down on a well-worn but comfortable armchair.

The inmates of Downing College enjoyed rather more spacious accommodation than the bed-sit world of old terraced houses. This was a proper sitting-room-cum-study; there were no bed-settees here.

'I share it with two others,' Andrew explained. 'Our bedrooms are through that door over there. I was lucky to be offered it. I had rooms outside last year. It was all right, but it's quieter in college, and much easier to concentrate.'

'You're in your final year, I believe. You're studying archaeology, are you?' Brenda asked.

'No, medieval history, actually. I've been doing archaeology purely out of interest,' MacGregor replied. His rugged features held a serious expression.

71

'What do you plan to do when you've got your degree?' Walsh inquired.

MacGregor shook his head. 'That I haven't really decided, always assuming I ever get a degree. I might consider teaching, or I could go into my father's engineering business.'

That was enough of the pleasantries. It was time to get down to business, Walsh decided. He would try to ruffle this young man's composure, and see how he reacted when under a little pressure and stress.

'Let's talk about cuneiform tablets. If I wanted to get hold of one, how should I set about it?' Walsh asked.

'I've no idea,' MacGregor replied bluntly.

'Well, where did you get yours?' Walsh demanded.

MacGregor frowned and his jaw jutted forward stubbornly.

'I'm sorry, Inspector, but I didn't put that tablet in the trench. I'd never seen it before, and neither do I know where it came from, or where it is now.'

'That's a pity,' Brenda suggested. 'It would have been a super joke. If Sir Gordon hadn't turned up unexpectedly, that tablet would have been booked in as a bona fide find. It would have been properly recorded, photographed, taken to a laboratory for decipherment, and might even have got into the newspapers, before anyone realised it was a hoax. An absolute cracker of a joke. One to be really proud of. Much better than frightening girls with plastic spiders or any of your other jokes,' Brenda posed quietly.

MacGregor's face reddened, and he swallowed hard.

'I don't play jokes like that,' he said firmly. 'I repeat. I didn't put that tablet in the trench. I'd never seen it be –'

'Yes, we heard all that, but you do play jokes. Are you denying that you planted the plastic spider, too?' Walsh demanded.

'That was different. Someone put it under my coat the day before. I thought it was one of the girls on the sieves, so I –'

'So you admit it?' Walsh prompted.

'The spider, yes, but not the tablet. I had nothing to do with that,' MacGregor denied hotly.

'Isn't it funny, though? The two people who happened to find the cuneiform tablet just happened to be punting up the river past Sir Gordon's garden, at the very moment he was killed. You didn't expect him to kick you out of the University, did you? So you went that night to reason with him. He argued, you hit him and ran off with the only real piece of evidence, the cuneiform tablet. It's so obvious, even a four-year-old could work it out. Why don't you admit it now? It'll be easier for you in the long run,' Walsh went on ruthlessly.

Andrew MacGregor's face was as white as a sheet, but he stuck doggedly to his story. 'I did not visit Sir Gordon that night, and I certainly didn't kill him. Where that tablet came from, or where it is now, I do not know.'


'Of course I'd heard about it, Sergeant,' Dr Charles Choosely said. His eyes looked serious, yet the lines on his face seemed to form the expression of a permanent smile. He was not a tall man, and he was a little stout, but he looked the part of an archaeologist, in his loose-fitting grey sweater and baggy black corduroy trousers.

'The students have been talking of nothing else for days. It's gossip mainly, of course, since most of them were too far away to hear what was actually said. It was a rather silly prank, I thought, but it's a pity Gordon didn't treat it as such, instead of flying off the handle as he did. Unlike him, really. Personally, I like to see a bit of high spirits in undergraduates. They're young, and if they're working their brains hard they need to let off steam in other ways. We were all like that at their age. Gordon ought to have shrugged it off. Naturally I asked him about it when I went round to his house the other day, but he was a bit curt, and said he didn't want to discuss it until he'd seen Professor Gladsbury.'

'Did you see the tablet yourself?' Reg Finch asked. Choosely's face was fascinating: that smile never went away, even when he was serious. No wonder he'd earned the nickname of the cheerful chappie Charlie Choosely, or was it just the cheerful Charlie Choosely? Reg couldn't remember.

'No. He never showed it to me. I wouldn't be able to tell what language it was anyway, nor would he. The study of those ancient Middle Eastern languages is a hell of a subject, best left to the specialist.'

'Does the level where the tablet was found tie up with the dates for cuneiform writing?'

'The carboniferous material found just above it hasn't been radio-carbon dated yet, but it probably isn't far off. However, there's no proper date for cuneiform writing in England. It just wasn't done here.'

'So you don't think there's a chance that the find was a genuine one then?' Reg asked quietly.

Choosely's constant smile twisted itself into a good representation of a sneer as he shook his head.

'Oh yes, there's a chance. About as much chance as you have of winning a jackpot first dividend on Littlewoods Pools – not just the once, mind you, but for each week of the year.'

'But the planting of that find must have been planned well in advance. After all, someone had to steal a tablet from somewhere, then wait until Fairbrother had excavated down to the appropriate level in the trench. That doesn't sound like spontaneous high spirits to me,' Reg stated.

'Neither does it to me, and I'm surprised that MacGregor is involved, and Fairbrother too. I'd always thought of them as being reasonably sane, down-to-earth types. As for them killing Gordon in order to retrieve the stolen tablet, that doesn't make sense either. Whatever Gordon may have said at the time, all that pair really had to do was to own up to the prank and to apologise profusely and profoundly. Then they'd have had their hands smacked and been given a verbal wigging. I can't see it would have been any worse than that. For them to have been sent down for such a thing would be far too draconian, in my opinion. Gordon getting murdered, though, puts a different complexion on things, I'm afraid.'

'It does indeed,' Reg agreed, 'and for that reason I'd like to talk to the students who regularly work on the site, so I'd appreciate a list of their names and colleges, if you'd be so kind. In addition to that, we'd like our forensic team to have a look at the spot where the tablet was found. You're in charge of the site now, I believe. I trust you'll have no objection. Would tomorrow morning at ten be convenient?'

Choosely hesitated, looked for a moment as though he would have liked to refuse, but then nodded. 'Certainly. I'll meet you there. Yes, I've taken over all Gordon's duties. Professor Gladsbury has the choosing of his assistants, you see, and he's promised to recommend me for the professorial chair itself, when he retires in a couple of years or so. That's something I never expected.'

'Did you not?' Reg said quietly. 'Do you by any chance own or ride a motor cycle, and where were you on Saturday evening, between seven and nine, if you don't mind my asking?'

Choosely shook his head. 'Not at all. I was at home, on my own, I'm afraid. My wife was out, and so were the boys. As for motor bikes, my eldest son's got one. I bought it for his sixteenth birthday.'


'So you don't think young MacGregor quite fits the bill as a vicious killer, then?' Walsh asked Brenda Phipps when they'd returned to his office.

'No, I wouldn't say that exactly,' she replied, 'but he's obviously very strong – if he'd swung an iron bar at Lignum's head, one blow would have been enough. Whoever did do it needed three, and even then only just managed to cave the skull in. No, he seemed a straightforward, decent enough young fellow to me.'

Walsh did not reply; he was reading the papers left on his desk by the C.C.'s secretary.

'We were looking for a motor cyclist,' he murmured. 'Now we might have dozens of them. Come on, Brenda. "Waste not a moment," and all that sort of thing – we're off again. Addenbrooke's Hospital, this time.'


'Mrs Samantha Leverington?' Walsh asked, smiling down at the young woman sitting with her back propped up by a pile of pillows on the hospital bed. Her undamaged right leg was encased in an elasticated stocking, while her left, still held together by the metal fixator, lay suspended in the narrow hammock. She wore a lacy cotton night-dress with short sleeves and a low neck. Prominent on one sleeve was a large pin-on badge showing a dog's head, with open jaws and large bared drooling teeth, under which was embroidered the name of a motor-cycle club.

'Yes, that's me,' she responded, her eyes brightening at the prospect of having the dour morning hospital routine broken for a while.

'This is Detective Constable Phipps,' Walsh went on, introducing Brenda, 'and I'm Detective Chief Inspector Walsh. We've come to talk to you about your accident. I know your injuries are serious, but the nurse says that you're healing remarkably well.'

Samantha's bright blue eyes widened, not a little surprised at the ranking of her visitors. 'That's because I'm fit. I do Akido, you know, or I did, before I came in here.'

'You need to be strong, to handle a powerful motor bike like yours,' Brenda murmured.

'Oh, I don't know. It's very well balanced, so it's not that difficult,' Samantha explained modestly. 'But you've come to see me about my accident, haven't you?

'Yes indeed,' Walsh smiled.

There was something appealing about this pretty blue-eyed girl with the long fair hair. She had a naïve innocence about her which made it difficult to think of her as an adult even, let alone as a married woman.

'But first,' he went on, 'an apology. Unfortunately the officer who came to the scene of your accident assumed that you would be transferred to the hospital in Huntingdon, so he sent the follow-up papers to the police station there. I'm not making excuses, but it did result in a charmingly well-constructed letter.'

Samantha gave a little chuckle, and rewarded Walsh with a widening of her deep blue eyes. 'You liked it, did you? I wasn't sure if I'd gone a bit over the top about the way the "I didn't see you" brigade get away with dangerous driving so easily. It is so much worse than merely speeding, isn't it?'

'We in the police force think so too. After all, you were lucky not to have been killed. Unfortunately all we can do is bring these people before the courts, then it's up to the judge to pass sentence according to the laws laid down by Parliament. Sometimes, like you, we feel that the punishment doesn't fit the crime. A letter like that to your MP might be more effective. We've made our recommendations to the Home Office often enough, that's all we can do,' Walsh admitted.

Samantha shrugged her slim shoulders reluctantly. 'These sort of accidents happen too often. Some drivers just don't look properly when they pull out, and it's not right if they get away with only a small fine. I know I'll get damages, but his insurance company will pay that. What about all the other costs he's caused? The doctor says I'm in here for at least three months, what about the cost of that? It would cost a small fortune if I were a private patient. The government's always moaning about how high the NHS funding is, yet they seem quite happy to bear the costs of the "I didn't see you" brigade.'

'Never mind,' Walsh said, 'as long as they get you fit and well again. That's the main thing, isn't it?'

'About your accident, Mrs Leverington,' Brenda interrupted impatiently. 'There isn't really very much that we need to ask you.' The Chief was always susceptible to a pretty female face, particularly a blue-eyed one, and Samantha's physical attractions were hardly much more concealed by her skimpy nightie than the bare flesh of that naked Australian girl had been by the hand-towel. Their visit had a serious purpose, and it was time they got on with it. This girl, who showed all the signs of being mildly scatterbrained, obviously hadn't been reading the local newspapers, for she seemed totally unaware that the man who had caused her accident was now dead.

'We've statements from witnesses,' Brenda went on determinedly, 'who say quite clearly that you were not to blame. In fact the driver of the Range Rover admitted to our officer that he hadn't seen you, and made a statement to that effect.'

Samantha clapped her hands together excitedly. 'Oh good. To be honest I don't remember that much about it. It happened so quickly. Did you know that that man actually phoned the ward here, wanting to come and see me? I said no, of course. I didn't want there to be any chance of him coming up against anyone from our club. They'd skin him alive, or worse,' she prattled on, proudly turning her shoulder to display the motor-cycle club badge of the dog with the bared teeth.

'They can get a bit rough, can they? The men in your club?' Brenda asked softly.

'I'll say. They don't call us the Mad Dogs for nothing, you know. There's no love lost between us and the "I didn't see you" brigade. There's many of them just missed an accident by the skin of their teeth, but there's others who've ended up like me, in hospital. You mustn't think that our boys are a nasty lot, though,' she explained, reaching out a trusting hand to touch Walsh's sleeve. 'You mustn't judge by the leathers and the beards, you know. Some of them can be a bit crude at times, but they're a marvellous bunch really. We do lots for charities, and visits to old people, that sort of thing.'

'You've had some of them here to visit you, I suppose?' Walsh asked, now looking more serious.

Samantha nodded vigorously. 'And there'll be more this weekend, now the news is getting about. Last Saturday the committee came. The chairman, the secretary and the treasurer, that is. It was lovely, just like a breath of fresh air. My husband was here as well, but he doesn't like them. He just can't see what nice people they really are.'

'That was last Saturday, was it? Did they stay long, these committee members?' Brenda asked silkily.

'They all left at much the same time, between half-seven and eight, the end of visiting hours.'

'Your committee members came on their bikes, I suppose? Would they have travelled together?'

'I doubt it. We don't go in for convoy riding in our club. So you'll be prosecuting this Sir Gordon Whats-his-name, will you?' she asked, gazing ingenuously up at Walsh's face.

He shook his head slowly. 'No, I'm afraid we won't be doing that. Sir Gordon Lignum has gone to a place where the whole conduct of his life will be examined, by a judge who will not be hampered by the laws of mere mortals. You obviously haven't read the local newspapers, Mrs Leverington. The man who knocked you off your motor bike is dead. He was killed by someone who ruthlessly beat him over the head with an iron bar. We're investigating his murder.'

Samantha Leverington first of all went rigid, then slowly sank back on to her pillows, her face very pale.

'When? When was he killed?' she whispered, obviously in some distress.

'Last Saturday evening, between seven thirty and nine thirty.'

'Oh my God!' she blurted out, before her fingers came up to cover her mouth. Yet in spite of that, the words that she breathed could be heard quite distinctly. 'I know they all like me, but not that much, surely? Not that much.'

6

The three members of the serious crime team had gathered together in Sidney Walsh's office.

It was not a meeting that had been planned.

Each had returned to write reports of the interviews and activities undertaken during the day. Such things were best done while events were still fresh in the mind. One could never be sure of what tomorrow might bring, and to be doing yesterday's paperwork first thing in the morning never did get a day off to a good start.

Since copies of those reports and statements needed to be entered into the case file, and the case file was kept in Walsh's office, it was not surprising that they should meet up and relax with a cup of coffee.

Reg Finch occupied his usual place on the far side of Walsh's desk, where he could stretch out his long legs, while Brenda Phipps slouched in one of the easy chairs by the window.

'You've seen Choosely then, Reg. What was he up to the night Lignum died?' Walsh asked.

'He says he was at home on his own. His wife was at her mother's and his boys were at a disco. I'll get young Alison Knott to check out his story, and I've a list of the students who worked on the site she can see as well. The rest of my day's been spent running round trying to find out which museum or faculty is missing a cuneiform tablet, but the way some of them keep their records, I might find out by next Christmas.' Reg tried hard to stifle a yawn.

'Do you think Choosely might have planted that tablet hoping Lignum might take it seriously, and so be made to look ridiculous?' Brenda inquired.

Reg pursed his lips thoughtfully. 'I wouldn't have thought it likely. No archaeologist worth his salt would readily accept a cuneiform tablet find in England as genuine, and Lignum wasn't daft. He'd never have put his career on the line over a thing like that.'

'So, if Choosely didn't plant it, it must have been put there by MacGregor and Fairbrother, or someone else?' Brenda stated with a frown.

Reg shrugged. 'We mustn't assume there is a link between the murder and the tablet.'

'Yet Lignum's killer must have taken the tablet away with him, since we haven't found it. That's a direct link, isn't it?' Brenda said emphatically.

'Yes, but what is more interesting is the question why Lignum didn't show the tablet to anyone, either to get a translation made or to find out where it had been stolen from. That's funny enough in itself to be suspicious,' Reg went on.

'Lignum might have been bribed by the developers to ensure that his archaeological report would clear the site quickly, but if he was going to keep quiet about the tablet anyway, why would the developers need to have him killed, Reg?' Walsh asked.

'I don't know. Maybe you'll find out more when you go to London tomorrow, but bear in mind that Lignum might have been so confused by the affair that he couldn't make up his mind what action to take. He couldn't talk it over with Professor Gladsbury, because he was away in Brighton,' Reg pointed out.

'Well, you're going to the Hinching Park site with Packstone in the morning. Hopefully Forensic will come up with something to clarify the situation. Now, I think we've spent enough time on that subject, so let's leave the clay tablet, and think about motor bikes,' Walsh decided.

'Choosely's son has a motor bike. It's a 95cc one, if I remember correctly. Choosely might have used that,' Reg announced.

Brenda smiled. 'Maybe, but we've got a whole club full of real bikers to go at, haven't we, Chief?'

'Samantha Leverington certainly thought so,' Walsh observed. 'Is that really likely, do you think?'

'She's got those blue-eyed, baby-doll looks that men often go gooey over,' Brenda said with some emphasis.

Reg Finch looked at her in surprise. 'Is she like that? I'd imagined her to be a hard case. Motor-bike clubs are predominantly male, and an attractive woman, even if she is married, must be subjected to a fair bit of sexual harassment.'

Brenda shrugged her slim shoulders. 'Maybe she's tougher than she looks, but it's more likely that they think of her as a sort of mascot – a young innocent sister, someone they can feel protective about. If one of their male members gets knocked off his bike they probably say "Tough luck," but if it's their blue-eyed, baby-doll mascot that gets hurt, then that's an entirely different matter. The Greeks went to war over Helen, didn't they? I can visualise the same sort of emotions being generated in this case, albeit on a smaller scale.'

Reg raised his eyebrows at what Brenda had said, and he thought of saying something sarcastic, but he changed his mind; it had dawned on him that both he and Walsh might feel much the same about Brenda, if it were she who was in danger – and she was no baby-faced mascot. One couldn't put that sort of thing into words, of course, so he contented himself by saying, 'There's no trouble but there's a woman involved.'

'In this case there was someone to go to war with,' Walsh said thoughtfully. 'A man named Lignum, and no difficulty finding out where he lived either, but a killing, Brenda? Surely a beating-up, a few broken bones would suffice, even for the most brutal motor biker.'

'How can you tell what it was meant to be? Violence creates its own marginal cases. Maybe Lignum's killer hit him harder than intended, or one time too many,' Brenda pointed out.

'You'd better take on this motor-bike angle, Brenda, but they're a clannish lot are bikers. If they get wind of the fact that we're investigating some of their members, they'll button their lips and we'll get nowhere. So it would be better if you can make your initial inquiries about the three names we have got without making it obvious what you're about. Do you think you can do that?'

Brenda nodded. 'These clubs all belong to a national federation. I think Alison Knott's brother is, or was, a biker. I'll ask her to have a chat with him, maybe he can advise us how to proceed.'

'Right! Now, Lady Lignum and her alibi. How have you got on?'

'She was at the start and finish of the rehearsal certainly, Chief, but as far as the middle is concerned, I can't pin her down. She's lost in the crowd.'

'Arthur Bryant can take over Beethoven's Ninth and Lady Lignum, while you get on with the motor-bike angle, and he can check out this solicitor Grant's story about being all Saturday evening at the golf club,' Walsh said as he looked down at his watch.

He'd been in no hurry earlier, but the time had flown by so quickly while they'd been talking. He'd have to go soon if he was to meet Gwen off the London train as he'd promised.

'We'll have to break off now,' he said, collecting his things together. 'We've all got plenty to get on with.'

82

'Are you both still here?' Reg asked, rather unnecessarily, when he found probationary Detective Constables Alison Knott and Arthur Bryant waiting in his office.

'In another ten minutes, we wouldn't have been,' Alison Knott admitted with a brief smile.

'When you two and the Chief Inspector get your heads together in a council of war there's no knowing when you'll finish,' Arthur Bryant added, 'but what is certain, is that when you do, you'll have plenty of work for us poor slaves.'

'A bit of hard work never did anyone any harm, Arthur. As a matter of fact I do have a nice simple job for you to do. You can take over the verification of Lady Lignum's alibi,' Brenda said, handing him a file.

'Isn't that complete yet? I thought she was with dozens of people at a concert rehearsal in the old Girls' High School, down Long Road.'

'So she was, but I can't yet tie her down for the whole period. In addition to that, the Chief wants you to get on your bike and up to the golf club, to check out solicitor Grant's story of what he was doing on the night Sir Gordon passed on.'

'It's alibi-checking for you too, Alison, I'm afraid,' Reg remarked. 'There's no file yet, but here's a copy of the report I made on my interview with the cheerful chappie Charlie Choosely, to start it off. Choosely's career prospects brightened significantly when Lignum's lights dimmed and went out. When you've done that, you can start interviewing the students on this list.'

'There's Mark Leverington, the accident victim's husband, to be checked out as well,' Brenda went on. 'He drives a Volvo, and a Volvo was seen near Lignum's house. You can do that too, Arthur, and give Alison a hand, she's more to do than you. Wake up, Arthur! I'm talking to you. You're dreaming again.'

'I was thinking about Beethoven's Ninth,' Arthur muttered thoughtfully. 'Lignum had doodled "B9" on his pad just before he was killed. He might have written that absent-mindedly, if he saw his wife's car come home when she should have been at the rehearsal.'

'He was in his study, working at his desk, Arthur,' Brenda pointed out patiently. 'He couldn't have seen anyone coming to the front door, or anyone coming to the french window in the sitting-room, for that matter. His killer probably crept up behind him, so he wouldn't have known who it was anyway.'

'This Mrs Choosely was at her mother's, was she? I'll have to check her out as well then, Reg,' Alison suggested. 'She might have been keen to advance her husband's prospects. The two boys – only fifteen and seventeen – aren't likely to be suspects, but nevertheless, I'll make sure they were at this disco place –'

'He was the ninth baronet. That's "B9" as well,' Arthur interposed.

'We know that, Arthur,' Brenda said snappily. 'Now, there's a new line for us to follow up – a motor-bike club called the Mad Dogs. I think you once said that your brother belonged to a club in Bedford, Alison. Have I got that right?'

'He used to, but I'm not sure if he still does. He rebuilt an old Matchless 500 twin a few years back, and got a lot of help from the club members,' Alison replied.

'I want to find out about three members of this Leverington girl's club committee, without creating a stir. They were in Cambridge the night Lignum was killed, you see, and Forensic have found traces of oil on the study carpet.'

'Lignum's cancer tumour turned out to be benign. That's another "B9",' Arthur pointed out seriously.

'Oh, do shut up about "B9"s, Arthur,' Brenda said angrily.

'I'm only trying to be helpful,' Bryant protested.

'Well, you're not.'

'I'll give my brother a ring now, Brenda, if you like,' Alison suggested hastily. 'If he's at home, you can have a chat with him.'


'That new carpet in the spare room looks very nice, Gwen,' Walsh said when he'd come downstairs. 'The fitter came on time, did he?'

'Dead on the dot, and he had it laid by nine thirty, so I didn't miss my train,' his wife replied shortly.

'All you need now is the new curtains, then everything will be fine and dandy for when your friends arrive,' Sidney responded brightly. Gwen wasn't looking too cheerful; perhaps she was just tired.

'They're not coming now – at least they're not coming when they said they were. Their daughter's had a car accident and is in hospital. She's not hurt badly, but they've had to cancel their flight for now,' Gwen said, looking a little woebegone.

'Oh dear. That's a shame. You'd been so looking forward to them coming. Never mind, how would you like to go to a concert instead? Beethoven's Ninth?' he asked.

'That'd be nice. Where?'

'Here at the Guildhall – the combined schools orchestra. We'll make up a party. Reg and Margaret are going to take two of their orphans, and there'll be Brenda and us. We can make a night out of it, and have a damned good meal afterwards,' Sidney suggested enthusiastically.

Gwen's face took on a smile, but she shook her head slowly.

'Two little eight-year-olds won't think much of being taken for a three-course dinner in a posh restaurant, I'm afraid, Sidney. Their idea of a treat will be beefburgers and chips in McDonald's. Still, it'll be a night out together. We don't seem to have had many lately, do we?'

# 7

Sidney Walsh took a taxi from London's Liverpool Street station to the tall glass and concrete Moorgate office block.

Inquiries had revealed that the cash found in Sir Gordon Lignum's safe, still in its bank wrappers, had been issued on a day during which there had been few significant cash withdrawals at that branch, and one of those had been by the developers of the Hinching Park site.

It was an unexpectedly direct link, and gave some substance to the suggestion that those involved in financing the project might have had a reason for the murder of Sir Gordon Lignum, but it was not a possibility that filled Walsh with any great enthusiasm. If the directors of such companies as this were to contemplate such a thing, they would hire a professional to do it for them. For Walsh to prove a link between them and any of those hoodlums in London who were ready to bash in any number of heads, would be difficult enough, even if he could find the right hoodlum.

The office reception area had wide white marble floors, a profusion of barrel-potted rubber tree plants, and a long-legged, mini-skirted blonde to enthuse male visitors with the radiance of her much-practised smile. However, it was a male menial who was summoned to escort Walsh to the upper reaches of the building, where he was expected.

'How can we help you, Chief Inspector? Naturally, we were very upset to hear of Sir Gordon's untimely death. We got on very well with him.' The man behind the desk wore a grey double-breasted suit and had facial features that were not dissimilar to those of Prince Charles, but there the resemblance ended, for he also had the foxy bright alert eyes of a thirty-year-old who was probably well on his way to becoming a City tycoon.

'I understand your company is developing the Hinching Park site,' Walsh stated, looking quickly round the room before sitting down. The office, and indeed the whole place, was bland of atmosphere. The feeling of space had been created by the lavish use of glass, but it was an empty, featureless, alien space. In such an environment Walsh found it difficult even to crease his face into a smile.

'I'd like you to tell me your contractual obligations in respect to the archaeological excavations, if you would be so kind, but before you do that, fill me in with some background about this company. Who owns it, what kind of land developments do you do, and what kind of sums are involved?'

The director smiled condescendingly down at the tips of his fingers.

'I'll keep it simple, if you don't mind. This company was set up to take advantage of the recession in the United Kingdom. Its backers are a consortium of fund managers from Hong Kong and the Middle East. The aim, to put it bluntly, has been to buy land from bankrupt speculators, or anyone else with loans they couldn't service, at rock bottom prices. Naturally, this land stock will be sold on again when the economy recovers. However, there are some sites worth developing now. Supermarkets are still falling over themselves to expand. Mind you,' he confided, 'that can't last for ever. They'll overreach themselves one day. So we must make hay while the sun shines. Hinching Park is an ideal site for an out-of-town supermarket, and when you get one of those interested then the DIY people, the furniture warehouse lot and the garden centre chains, they all want a piece of the action as well. How much is involved altogether, including the nearby housing development? I'm not sure if I should tell you that, but you'll get little change from six or seven million.'

'What motivates you, personally, to try and generate big profits for a group of faceless investors, who are probably rolling in money anyway?' Walsh inquired somewhat unenthusiastically.

The other looked surprised. 'Why, more money, of course. That's what life's all about, isn't it? I have a good salary, naturally, but I can double or treble that from my share of the profits. So I suppose you could say I'm working for myself really.'

'And your archaeological obligations at Hinching Park?' Walsh prompted.

'Planning regulations are pretty standard everywhere in the country these days. We are required to fund a site survey by suitably qualified archaeologists, to ensure that none of Britain's historical heritage is destroyed without having been properly recorded. That's fair enough. We don't disagree with that in principle. We've made arrangements with Cambridge University to do the survey at Hinching Park as part of their tuition programme. They knew from records and aerial photographs that there had been a Saxon village on the site, but it wasn't one of particular importance.'

'So you've made payments direct to the University, then. Were they in cash or by cheque?' Walsh asked.

'By cheque, of course.'

'Then why was Sir Gordon Lignum given a thousand pounds in cash?'

The developer looked startled at that. He blinked, frowned and drummed his fingers on his desk top for a moment. Then he got up and went to stare out through the double-glazed window panes that so effectively cut out the noise of London's traffic in the street below.

'That money was for miscellaneous site expenses,' he said coldly. 'Students' grants are not generous, and that sum was an *ex gratia* contribution by the company towards meals and refreshments when they were working on the site.'

'So it wasn't given specifically to Sir Gordon, as an inducement for him to make sure that your site did not turn out to be of historical importance?'

'Of course not – and I don't like your implication that we would resort to bribery.' His eyes had narrowed menacingly, and gone was any sign of a friendly manner.

For some strange reason Walsh found that he could now smile pleasantly without effort.

'I'm pleased to hear that. Were you aware that a few days before his death Sir Gordon had made an unexpectedly important find dating from about 1250 BC? One which could well make your site one of national importance? How will you and your directors feel about a possible delay of a year or two while the whole area is intensively excavated?'

The other's lips twisted into what was undoubtedly meant to be a sneer, but the hostility in his eyes was intensely real and very genuine.

'What a load of bloody nonsense. This baked clay tablet with cuneiform writing on it? We've heard about it. Sir Gordon made it quite clear at the time that he thought it was a practical joke perpetrated by one of his students; and just in case you're interested, I've already taken advice from some pretty eminent people at the British Museum. It is their unanimous view that the idea of any such Middle Eastern artefact being found in this country is utterly ludicrous, and they would be prepared to say so, should an inquiry be necessary.'

'So, you're prepared for any kind of eventuality, are you?'

'Naturally,' he replied smugly. 'You don't get to run multi-million pound ventures in the City of London if you can't keep one jump ahead of the opposition, or if you're chicken-hearted or squeamish.'


The head of the forensic department, Dr Richard Packstone, had arrived at Hinching Park in one of the Cambridgeshire Constabulary's four-wheel-drive Land Rovers.

Possibly he'd thought that the vehicle's off-road ability to grind its way over precipitous mountain tracks, or wallow through glutinous monsoon mud, might well be needed when driving over Huntingdon's flat grassland. However, he managed to negotiate the level dusty track without any apparent difficulty.

He'd dressed for the occasion in a khaki drill outfit, and looked more like a Victorian explorer who'd forgotten his white pith helmet than a modern forensic scientist on a murder inquiry.

Reg Finch and the others came over with a site plan to spread out on the Land Rover's hot bonnet.

'There's been no human habitation on this site since the Saxon villagers were kicked out in Norman times. That was when the first manor house was built, way over there,' Dr Charles Choosely explained, pointing vaguely to the north. 'No doubt the Saxons smelled, or they spoiled the view. So they had to go.'

'Wouldn't they have been Danish settlers here, when the Normans came, rather than Saxon?' Reg Finch asked tentatively.

Choosely's fixed smile broadened.

'You've a point there. When one thinks of the Dark Ages one does tend to talk of Jutes, Britons, Angles, Saxons, Vikings and Danes, but when the Normans invaded those niceties get forgotten, and the indigenous population all gets lumped together as Anglo-Saxons, or Saxons for short,' he answered, but by then it was a somewhat absent-minded reply since his interest had been taken by the sight of all the equipment Packstone's assistant was unloading from the back of the Land Rover. 'Good Lord,' he went on, now shaking his head. 'I haven't seen so much stuff since I worked on the Sutton Hoo site survey in the eighties. All these electronics, sonic things and magnetometers. An archaeologist has to be an expert in everything these days.'

Packstone scratched his grey-haired head and gave a wry smile. 'Our searches are probably more limited than yours. What we're looking for is more clearly defined: bodies buried in back gardens, murder weapons thrown into bushes, that sort of thing. Modern equipment has been concentrated and miniaturised, so it's much easier to use.'

'Would you get the covers off "K" trench, please?' Choosely asked a group of students who were sitting on the grass by the site hut.

'It's been sealed like this since the tablet was found, has it?' Packstone asked, waving a hand at the long narrow tarpaulins that were now being unhooked from steel restraining pegs.

'That's right. That's what Sir Gordon instructed us to do,' one of the students, a thin-faced bespectacled young man, announced. 'No one's been down there to work since then, I can assure you of that. I've been here all the time.'

Nevertheless, when the tarpaulins had finally been cleared away it was quite obvious to all those who stood looking down into the trench that the young man was completely and utterly wrong.

The bottom of trench 'K' looked like a ploughed field. Someone had been working there, not with a tiny trowel and brush, but with a spade. The ground was so badly churned up that clearly the opportunity to ascertain whether the missing cuneiform tablet had been found in soil undisturbed for centuries had gone – for ever.

Surprisingly none of the viewers said a word, and perhaps that silence was the most expressive of comments.

Reg Finch put his briefcase down and sat on the edge of the trench in the sunshine. This line of inquiry into the murder of archaeologist Sir Gordon Lignum had suddenly developed in a way that had been unexpected. On reflection, of course, and with the benefit of hindsight, perhaps he should have treated the examination of this site with a greater sense of urgency than he had. He'd expected Packstone's examination of the trench to resolve the question of whether the cuneiform tablet had been placed there as a practical joke. However, someone had decided to destroy the evidence, and the most obvious person to gain from that action would be young Andrew MacGregor, or was that too simple an explanation?

'So!' came a soft voice from behind him. 'The man who holds the key that opens any door has, like Napoleon, met his Waterloo. All the Queen's horses and all the Queen's men, you included, will never put the bottom of that trench together again.'

Reg Finch turned his head and looked up at the rather cynical features of the young man he'd met in the museum, when he'd called to see Professor Gladsbury. This morning though, instead of the lank dark hair being pulled back into a pony tail, it hung untidily down to his shoulders.

'Did you get your pottery shards sorted out?' Reg asked quietly, ignoring the verbal challenge.

'Two defeated me,' came the reply.

'That's not bad. Tell me, what's the view of the students about all this? Was MacGregor the one who planted the cuneiform tablet in that trench as a practical joke, or not?'

'Opinion is divided. It's about fifty-fifty, I'd say,' the young man replied thoughtfully. 'However, that's not the really important question, is it? Much more to the point is, did that insignificant pawn named Tiny MacGregor kill the Queen's knight, Sir Gordon? The girls are positive that he didn't, but the men are not so certain – they think, perhaps three to two, that he did.'

'Interesting,' Reg mused. 'What's your name?'

The young man cocked his head sharply to one side. 'My name's Isaiah. See, one eye's higher than the other,' and he laughed and moved away.

Reg's foot banged against the side of the trench as he pushed himself to his feet, sending a few stones rattling to the bottom.

'Would you mind not doing that,' Charles Choosely muttered absent-mindedly. 'It contaminates the bottom area when you knock material down from more recent layers.'

'Sorry,' Reg said, rather shamefaced.

'Well, there's not much we can do here now, Reg,' Packstone remarked casually. 'Give me a hand to get my stuff back in the Land Rover. Then we'd better sit down and work out our next move.'


'The developers have a lot at stake, Reg,' Brenda suggested. 'They're effectively signing a blank cheque if the site does turn out to be of historical importance.'

Reg Finch nodded. 'The risk is greater in places like London or Colchester. You'd expect fewer problems on a green field site like this one. However, if they did have that trench dug up, they're not out of trouble yet.'

'How come?' Walsh asked.

'Well, the provisional dating of that carboniferous layer where the tablet was found is *circa* 1250 BC, give or take a hundred years or so. So, if one stands back to view the problem dispassionately, that information alone provides sufficient grounds to warrant further investigation, or it does in my opinion. I couldn't dictate matters to Dr Choosely, of course, but I could twist his arm a little. So I told him that since MacGregor was on our suspect list, we considered the clarification of whether the tablet was a joke, or authentic, was of paramount importance to our murder inquiry; and that if he didn't extend the excavations to either side of trench

92

"K", to seek some corroborative evidence, then our forensic department would do it for him.'

Walsh's eyebrows rose sharply in surprise at that, and he looked positively alarmed. The University was very sensitive when it came to its relationships with other civil organisations, and it would look askance, as much out of principle as for any other reason, at anything that might encroach on its hallowed independence. Reg sounded as though he'd been highly dictatorial, in which case there might well be trouble ahead. When you wanted the University to do something, a reasoned and logical approach was best: one showing due respect for their learned institutions, and that only after a quiet chat for guidance with someone like Professor Hughes at Downing College. Like ancient rival Scottish clans, the Town and Gown brigades eyed each other with watchful suspicion, quite ready to see in the most impotent of actions an horrendous attack on their dignity and authority.

'Why the hell did you have to say it like that, Reg?' Walsh blurted out anxiously. 'Lord, the C.C.'ll do his nut if there's trouble. Besides, I doubt if Packstone's lot have the time, even if he was prepared to do it.'

'Don't panic, boss,' Reg said with a broad grin. 'Packstone and I had it all worked out. It was only a bluff. Choosely had to take it on whether he liked it or not, didn't he? With Fairbrother and MacGregor denying it was a practical joke, the University has to get to the bottom of the problem, one way or another. We've merely brought the decision forward. Besides, there was another reason for doing it that way – it gave us the chance to insist on having our representative there while the crucial part of the new excavation was being carried out.'

'And that representative is you, I suppose, Reg,' Brenda chipped in sarcastically. 'Nice work, sitting about all day watching those girl students take more and more of their clothes off as they work in the sun. They don't wear a lot to start with, most of them.'

'I hadn't thought of that, Brenda, but yes, I'll volunteer for the job,' Reg admitted cheerfully.

'I trust you also insisted there should be a proper security guard kept on the site at night this time?' Walsh asked.

'Well, no, boss. I didn't bring that subject up, as a matter of fact,' Reg replied with an even broader grin on his face. 'I thought to myself that if they didn't post a guard, then there was just the possibility that someone might come back one night, to mess the site up again. Then, who knows, maybe we might have someone lying in wait to catch him in the act.'

'An ambush, by heavens. That's good thinking. I like it,' Walsh said, now looking much more relaxed.

'If you're planning that for this weekend, Reg, you can count Alison Knott and me out. We're off to a motor-bike rally,' Brenda announced.

'You've seen Alison's brother then?' Walsh asked.

'Yes. As we decided, it wouldn't be wise to alert the Mad Dog club by interviewing those three who visited Samantha Leverington on the night Lignum was murdered, so I thought that our groundwork might best be done at a motor-bike rally. They're social occasions really. They meet up for a good time and a natter with others of like interests. The pair of us ought to be able to chat around and find out if the feelings against the "I didn't see you" brigade are sufficiently strong for some of them to play executioner to their own kangaroo court. I'll pop into Addenbrooke's first, though, and have another word with the Leverington girl. I might learn something more from her that could be useful. You do realise that those three committee members live near the Hinching Park excavation site, Chief?'

'I had noticed, and so too does Mark Leverington, Samantha's husband,' Walsh added.

'I don't think he's our murderer, Chief. Alison says that when he left the hospital that night, he gave his mother-in-law a lift home, and stayed with her until nearly ten o'clock, so it couldn't have been his Volvo that was seen near Grantchester Meadows,' Brenda pointed out.

'How will you go to your rally, Brenda? Those sort of people can usually spot coppers a mile off,' Reg pointed out.

'Alison has been on one with her brother, so her face is known. However, I'll go pillion with her brother, and she'll go with one of his friends, but we'll chaperone each other and share a tent. The rally's on the east coast, at Great Yarmouth.'

'Have you got the right sort of gear?' Walsh asked.

'That's no problem. Alison's brother knows what we're up to, of course, there was no way of getting around that, so he'll be able to make sure we meet the right people. It's funny, Alison's on the stocky, well-built side, but her brother's tall and skinny, like Reg.'

# 8

Detective Constable Brenda Phipps pushed through the double entrance doors of Addenbrooke's broken bones ward, and strolled casually along to the bay which housed Samantha Leverington's bed.

'Hello! You came with the Chief Inspector, didn't you? I can't say I expected to see you again,' Samantha said with a welcoming smile.

'I can't say I expected to see you again, either,' Brenda admitted, perching herself on the arm of the easy chair next to the bed, 'but I just happened to be in the area, so I thought I'd pop in and say hello. How's it going?'

'Terrible,' Samantha scowled. 'I'm not allowed off this bed, and I just can't do anything for myself. I feel so helpless. I want to be up and doing things. I don't exactly know what things, mind you, but anything would be better than just lying here.'

'I think I know how you feel,' Brenda said quite truthfully, 'and by the time you're mobile again the winter will be here, and you'll have missed all this year's motor-bike rallies.'

'I know, and it's just not fair. I really do enjoy them. Mind you, I can only go when my husband's off rock climbing. What he sees in that I don't know. I went with him a few times and I was bored out of my mind. I prefer rallies, even if I have to go on my own,' Samantha explained.

'Don't you find it a bit difficult, with all those men?'

'Not really. They're not so bad, when you get to know them. Mind you, I set things out pretty clearly when I first joined the club. I made a speech to introduce myself, and I told them I was married, and I wasn't looking for sex or part-time men or anything like that. I just liked motor bikes. If they could accept that, then I was happy to be friends with anyone and everyone.'

'Good for you. Did it work?'

'There was one fellow, at the first rally I went to, Northampton it was, he tried to get fresh, but the others were keeping an eye on me, for I'd hardly had time to give a screech, when Jim, he's the butcher, and Graham, he's the solicitor, were both there. What they did or said to him I don't know, but I never saw him again.'

'What about the language? I should think it gets pretty crude.'

Samantha grimaced. 'Yes, and I don't like that, but it's not so bad now they've got used to me. Funnily enough, I think they're pleased in a way when I'm around and they don't have to swear. A lot of them are only acting the part of macho men, and when I'm there they can relax and be themselves. Some of them are lonely too, you know, but they find they can chat to me because I take them as they are. Jim's a bit like that. He's good fun when his mates are with him, but on his own he goes all shy and quiet. I know he was married once, but I don't think he's got a girlfriend now.'

'And violence?'

'Not over me,' Samantha said emphatically. 'There's some fights occasionally, of course, you'd expect that with men, but it's more often with local lads who've had too much to drink.'

Brenda went away thinking much more highly of Samantha Leverington than she had at their first meeting. Apparently there was an active brain behind that childish baby-doll face.


'So, until she got her teeth into Sir Gordon Lignum, your Lady Ingrid was nothing better than a tart – a common bloody tart,' the C.C. said scornfully, and tossed the report from the Swedish police across the desk to where Walsh sat.

Walsh thought of the woman's attractive face and superb figure, and pursed his lips.

'Why my Lady Lignum?' he asked reflectively. 'But whatever she was, you can hardly describe her as common.'

'All right then. A high-class bloody tart.'

'Brenda thought she was a hard case,' Walsh muttered as he picked the report up and started to read it for himself.

'Did she so? Smart girl, that Brenda of yours,' the C.C. grunted.

Ingrid Moulmark had not finished her arts course at Stockholm University, having presumably found the ancient trade of selling sexual favours more interesting or more financially rewarding. She had worked the hotels and casinos of Stockholm in the summer, and those in Rome or the south of France during the winter, so the report read, until a few years ago. Perhaps the life of a high-class tart had disadvantages, or possibly the varied excitement of such an existence faded after a while. Whichever it was, marriage to Sir Gordon Lignum had presumably offered a more attractive alternative. It would be interesting to know whether Lignum had been aware, at the time, of his wife's occupation. Walsh had formed the opinion that Lignum had been one of those academic types who was so tied up with his interest in the past that he was somewhat detached from the real world about him. Yet it was difficult to believe that a man of his years would not be able to recognise the kind of person Ingrid was when he met her. On the other hand, she was attractive enough, and probably skilled enough too, to generate in men that most mindless of emotions – infatuation. That was a self-hypnotic mental state which rendered people utterly blind to the most obvious, even repulsive, faults in another. If that had been the case, there was no good looking for logical explanations, they wouldn't exist.

'Are we going to sit here staring at each other all day, Sidney?' the C.C. demanded impatiently. 'I've got other things to do, even if you haven't.'

Walsh jerked himself out of his thoughts, and slipped the Swedish report into the front of his file; there would be time for further reflections on it later.

'It was some years ago that he married her. It's difficult to see how her past activities on the Continent could have anything to do with recent events here in Cambridge,' he commented. 'However, that doesn't mean to say that they might not. But let's move on to other things. I've had reports come through from the schools of these two students, MacGregor and Fairbrother.'

'Good. They're the prime suspects in this case, in my opinion. Either of them, or both together.'

'Well, MacGregor's school in Stirling considers him to be hard-working and intelligent, but he's got a bit of a temper, apparently, if he's pushed too far. He's been involved in a few fights. The other one, Melissa Fairbrother, wasn't an easy pupil either, until she set her mind to getting her A levels, but that was mostly because of the strictness of the rules in a school for young ladies, and there was no indication of violence in her behaviour.'

The C.C. shrugged his shoulders. 'That's not a lot to go on. Kids often only conform to the standards required by their immediate surroundings. Send them to a place like Cambridge and give them a bit of freedom, and they can go really wild and do stupid things. I did, when I was that age. I called it high spirits then, of course. Nowadays I'd call it bloody idiotic behaviour,' he admitted, grinning broadly.

'New Zealand have come through with a report about Lignum's cousin, the new baronet. His name's Adrian, and he's a budding lawyer in Wellington. Aged twenty-six, unmarried and has never left his native land before. Now he's on his way here for the funeral.'

'If he was on the other side of the world at the time, he couldn't have bumped his cousin off, could he? Anything else of interest to report?'

'I've asked the Fraud Section to check out the transactions of Lignum's trust. If Grant, the solicitor, has been dipping his fingers in the trust's till, that might provide a motive for murder if Lignum had suddenly got wind of it. Grant says that the Lignums were good friends of his, but I had the feeling that it was Ingrid who was the big attraction. He's good looking and a bit of a womaniser, I think. I doubt if anyone in skirts is very safe when he's on the prowl.'

'Or anyone in trousers, if Lignum's wife wanted to put herself about.'

'Maybe, but if she did, she was very discreet. There's not a hint of scandal from the people she knew at the Polytechnic.'

'I can't see a tart like her settling down easily to domestic life in Cambridge. You delve deeper, Sidney. Old habits die hard, she'll have been practising the arts of her ancient trade on someone somewhere. Right, anything else?'

'Only that Phipps and Knott are off this weekend on a motor-bike rally in Great Yarmouth. They're out to make some surreptitious inquiries about the members of the motor-bike club that girl Leverington belongs to. Maybe one of those felt angry enough to beat Lignum up – and went too far,' Walsh explained.

'Excellent! Well worth following up, and you're wise to keep your inquiries under cover at this stage. If the motor-bike fraternity found that you were interested in one of their number, they'd all clam up tight and you'd have a devil of a job finding anything out. Mind you, one can't help feeling a bit of sympathy with them, about the "I didn't see you" brigade. Nevertheless, they're a funny lot themselves, are motor-bikers. Short-tempered, and not afraid to swing their fists about. Have you told the Norfolk police that two of ours will be working on their territory over the weekend?' the C.C. asked.

Walsh shook his head. 'Not yet, but I will.'

'Right! Now, have you sussed out the meaning of those letters and numbers Lignum had written on that bit of paper? They could be important.'

'You mean, "B9" and "K9"? Well, "K9" was the position in the trench where the tablet was found. As for "B9", it could be Beethoven's Ninth or the fact that he was the ninth baronet. Young Bryant thinks it might even mean benign. Lignum's cancer tumour turning out to be B9. Get it?'

'Christ! Do I look stupid, Sidney?' the C.C. growled.

Walsh merely shrugged. 'Maybe Lignum took a break from writing his report on the excavations at Hinching Park, and maybe doodled while sorting his thoughts out later.'

'You've too many maybes, Sidney. It's high time you started to eliminate some of them,' the C.C. suggested caustically.

'That's just what I'm trying to do, but there's not a lot to go on as yet, is there?'


'We've some good news, boss,' Reg Finch said when Walsh returned to his office. 'Some of the things taken from Lignum's house have turned up.'

'Where?'

'Enfield – North London.'

'Ring them back, then. Tell them we're on our way.'

'No need. I told them to expect us in the next hour or so.'


'They was in these here two plastic bags, you see, in me garden shed,' the little round-faced man said, blinking his puffy eyes as though to express his utter amazement. 'I found them this morning, and I high-tailed it straight down here to the cop-shop. Me, I don't know nothing about them. Someone's planted them on me, for God's sake.'

The Enfield CID Inspector leaned back in his chair and chuckled loudly.

'He came in flapping his wings so hard it was a wonder he didn't take right off and loop the loop. Playing the upright honest citizen don't come easy to a hardened old lag like Peter Ellis here. What is it? Three times or four times you've been put inside for receiving stolen property?'

Ellis scowled irritably, then forced his tight lips into a grin. 'Three times I've been wrongly convicted, but I'm going straight now, I am. I don't want no trouble, not with you lot, anyway.'

'Let me get this straight,' Sidney Walsh insisted, frowning deeply and staring at all the highly collectable items spread out on the desk. 'You say you found this stuff in your garden shed, and you've no idea who put it there?'

'S'right, mate. I haven't a clue,' Ellis replied perkily.

'What he really means is that he don't know this A.M. chap who signed the note that was in the bag. Even his tiny mind was wide awake enough to smell a rat at that,' the Inspector explained, pushing the piece of paper over the desk to his visitor.

Walsh picked it up and read the words again.

'Hold these for me. See you Friday night, late,' and it was signed 'A.M.'. The handwriting was crude, probably written with the left hand by a right-handed person, or vice versa, and the paper was lined, torn from a wire-ringed notebook, probably of the shorthand kind.

'You don't know an A.M. then?' Walsh asked.

Ellis shook his head vigorously. 'I knows an A.M. but it ain't him. . . .'

'. . . Because he's inside doing a two-year stretch. We put Andy Morris away only three or four weeks ago,' the Enfield Inspector interrupted.

'Do you know a Molly O'Brien by any chance, Ellis?' Walsh asked.

Ellis blinked, frowned and shook his head. 'Never heard of her.'

'Your back garden,' Reg Finch asked, 'easy to get at, is it?'

'Sure, dead easy. The back passage runs behind all the houses, like.'

Walsh drummed his fingers on the desk. It rather looked as though, if they wanted to find out who A.M. was, they'd have to do a bit of late night-time vigil, watching for whoever came to visit this Peter Ellis on Friday night. He'd been assuming that it was Lignum's killer who had taken the items that now lay on the desk before him. That wasn't necessarily so, but it was likely.

'If you're thinking what I think you're thinking,' the Inspector said calmly, 'let me make my position quite clear. I'll do everything I can to help, but you'll have to run the show yourselves. My lot are right up to here,' he explained, raising his hand to the top of his forehead.

'Here, you ain't planting no coppers in my house. No way,' Ellis cried out determinedly, in some alarm. 'I've done my bit, bringing this stuff in. If you want to pick this A.M. up, you'll have to do it outside in the street. I'm not getting involved. No, I'm not. I've my reputation with the neighbours to consider,' he went on, jutting his jaw out stubbornly.

'This A.M. says "late". What time do you shut up shop, Ellis? Midnight? One o'clock?'

'I'm going straight now, I tell you. I won't have no visitors Friday night, and I'll be in bed by one. You can pick up anyone who comes, I don't care,' Ellis said reluctantly.

'You'll get the word round to your mates to keep well clear of your place, will you? Still, that'll suit us. I can let you have one of our vans, but I can spare only one local man for a late-night surveillance operation like this,' the Inspector offered.

Walsh nodded understandingly. With Brenda Phipps and Alison Knott away sleuthing the motor-cycle rally, and Arthur Bryant keeping a surreptitious eye on the archaeological site near Huntingdon, that only left Reg and himself. This whole set-up smelled mighty fishy, but if the murderer did keep his appointment with the fence, Peter Ellis, and walked into a successful ambush, then maybe, tonight, the whole case could be cleared up, wrapped up and tied up.

'We'll manage,' he said confidently.


# 9


The broad grassy meadow behind the pub on the northern outskirts of Great Yarmouth was dotted with lightweight tents of a variety of hues, and a similar number of equally varied and colourful motor bikes.

In places tussocks of spiky marsh grass suggested areas of damper ground and these were wisely avoided by the early comers. By and large though, it was an ideal temporary campsite, for the next field contained one of the many caravan parks common on this part of the east coast, and access to its solidly built toilet blocks, through gaps in a thorny hedge and over a ditch on simple plank bridges, was an additional luxurious advantage.

The weather was fine at the moment, and the forecast for the weekend was fair. Broken cloud scudded across the darkening evening sky, driven by the fresh east wind coming off the North Sea, which could just be seen as a faint grey line in the distance, away over the far side of the caravan park, beyond the long line of grass-topped sand dunes that guarded the beach northwards to Caistor and beyond.

Matthew Knott had ridden his elderly but immaculate motor bike from Cambridge to Yarmouth with a considerable degree of caution and care. One reason was that he hadn't used it for many months, and he was not prepared to take any risks that might end up causing damage to the machine that he had spent so much time and effort restoring. There was another reason: he felt distinctly uneasy with this policewoman friend of his sister's. She was pleasant enough, and attractive enough too, but there was something about her large brown eyes that unnerved him. Often they held an expression which was disarmingly soft and smiling, but at other times they seemed the source of invisible laser beams that bored inquisitively into his very soul, searching to read his innermost thoughts.

So, by the time that pair arrived, the general layout of the campsite had already been formulated. Club members naturally chose to pitch their tents as near to their friends and comrades as they could.

However, Alison Knott, travelling earlier and faster with her brother's friend, had arrived soon enough to influence that layout by staking a site for herself close to the tents of Samantha Leverington's club members.

'Well done,' Matthew whispered conspiratorially to his sister as he set about unloading the camping gear from his motor bike.

It was no problem setting up a tent in the gathering darkness, for there were many friendly hands ready to assist if needed.

It was a pity she was there on business, Brenda thought, but even so, there was no reason why this mightn't be made into a pleasant weekend.

Tomorrow there would be organised events, both social and technical, the local club playing host, but for this evening, nothing specific was planned.

Inevitably there was a gradual drifting off to the lighted convivial atmosphere of the pub. Good timing enabled Matthew's group to mingle with the members of the Mad Dog club while fetching drinks from the bar, and it seemed natural for them to sit together at the same large table, outside in the garden area behind the pub's car-park. That area was well lit by several overhead yellow floodlights, which gave a warm glow that was somewhat at variance with the cool onshore breeze. However, since most of those seated at the wooden tables still wore their leather outfits, it was doubtful whether they noticed the sudden fall in temperature.

It was a cheerful scene, and a crowded one, out there in the garden, but it was even more crowded in the main building. The hubbub of conversation, liberally sprinkled with laughter, was just what one might have expected from a gathering of friends and acquaintances with much to talk about.

Certainly it was a scene that brought pleasure to the eyes of the pub landlord, who had taken a few minutes to get out from behind his bar, to stretch his legs and collect empty glasses from the tables in the garden. Such events as this brought him the certainty of a good weekend trade, not only from the sale of liquid refreshment, but also from the snacks and cooked meals he was offering.

Brenda thought things were going very well indeed. Already she and Alison had been introduced to the three men who had visited Samantha Leverington on the night Sir Gordon Lignum had been murdered. They were obviously very close friends and of much the same age. Graham Spencer, the solicitor, was a stoutish, round-faced man with dark hair. Giles Partridge, the accountant, was taller, but lean and with fair hair. They were both on the far side of the table, where Brenda could study their faces without making it too obvious what she was doing. They were relaxed and friendly, and there was no hint in the features of either that might suggest they were vicious killers. The third of that trio she could not keep under observation, because he was sitting right beside her. Jim Vine, the butcher, was a stocky, well-built man with thin reddish hair and a rather sad introverted face. He responded to the general conversation sociably enough, but he lacked the verbal flair of his two friends. He'd positioned himself to be near her as soon as he'd learned she was single and unattached, but having done so, he was making little attempt to make himself agreeable. Some men were like that: desirous of female company yet unable, because of inhibitions, to relax and be natural. He was certainly a fellow with a few complexes, and it looked as if it was going to be hard work and no pleasure for her to try and work out just what those complexes were. She looked enviously over at Alison, who was now engaged in an animated conversation with the solicitor and the accountant. It was noticeable that those two frequently glanced over at Jim Vine beside her. Were they concerned or worried at what he might be getting up to?

'Ever had an accident, yourself?' Brenda asked.

The man beside her cleared his throat.

'Several times,' he admitted, while studying his half-filled beer glass.

'Any broken bones?'

'Not me.'

It wasn't going to be at all easy, playing the part of a spy in the enemy's camp. Alison was clearly doing far better than she was, from what she could hear of their conversation.

'Isn't it a lovely evening? So peaceful and quiet,' Brenda said tamely, and indeed it was, but that was to change so quickly that most of them there were taken completely by surprise.

A wild-eyed, leather-clad group suddenly came charging into the garden area from the car-park, knocking into the tables, upsetting glasses, pushing and shoving those who were on their feet, and generally shouting abuse as they did so.

Those people seated nearest to the gap in the hedge leading to the campsite were quickly up and away, but others found that extricating themselves from the chairs and tables could not be accomplished speedily, and they were the ones to become the victims of the punch-throwing, glass-throwing newcomers.

Jim Vine was quickly on his feet, and he pushed Brenda behind him, obviously with the intention of protecting her from the troublemakers, but that brave action did not last long. A swinging blow from a heavy quart-sized glass tankard caught him just behind his left ear and he crumpled silently to the ground.

Brenda was now directly in the firing line, and prompt action was needed for her own self-preservation as well as for her erstwhile protector, now lying prone at her feet. The glass-swinger raised a boot to kick at Jim Vine's head, so she quickly threw out her fist in a short sharp straight left-arm jab, which caught the young rioter right in the eye. That jab appeared to do no significant damage, but it did serve to concentrate the kicker's frenzied attention solely on his new lightweight opponent.

Brenda was hemmed in by the table and was astride Vine's unconscious body. Both restricted her freedom of movement, forcing her to stand and parry some of the blows aimed at her, and duck and weave to avoid others. The pain from those that found a mark made her coldly angry, and at the first opportunity she went on the offensive.

She caught the man's wrist, deftly twisted her body, and heaved. By rights her opponent should have been sent somersaulting forward to the ground, but there just wasn't enough room for her to make that throw fully effective, and all she achieved was to temporarily wind the man as he landed with a thud on the table top. Obviously she needed to revise her too sophisticated tactics for something cruder. So she twisted the man's arm as high up behind his back as she could with one hand, then grabbed at his hair with the other, and tried to demolish the table into its component planks, using his head as a hammer.

She was dimly aware that other battles were raging around her. There was more space in which to move now; obviously some people had managed to retreat, but with Vine still lying helpless at her feet, there was no way she could follow them.

She'd got herself into a bit of a fix, she realised, and frankly her arms were starting to tire of the table demolition business. Unfortunately her opponent was strong and completely impervious to pain, or perhaps he enjoyed having his head bashed monotonously on to solid wood, for he showed no sign of giving up, and indeed he was fighting back by raking her shins with the heels of his boots.

In a one-to-one encounter, with space to move, her skill and ability would have overcome this character long ago, but in close-quarter fighting like this, it was stamina and physical strength that mattered. She could, of course, bring things to a speedy end with one quick back-hand chop to the base of his neck, but with that there was a good chance of actually killing him, and she dared not take the risk. As it was, she was already experiencing that sick feeling in the pit of her stomach that presaged panic, for her arms were beginning to weaken, and if this young thug got the upper hand, she would be in for a real pounding.

The hands that grabbed her arms from behind made her react in sheer desperation. Having one opponent was bad enough; two would be a disaster. So she abandoned Jim Vine, let go of her first assailant and jerked quickly to one side. That wrenched those unknown hands from her arms, and gave her enough space to deal with her new opponent, if she still had the strength. She half turned into a crouch as she grabbed at his wrist, then with a quick twist and a shoulder heave, this one was sent hurtling forward quite satisfactorily, with enough impetus to slide gracefully over the table and thence to the ground on the far side.

A blue silver-badged helmet appeared from nowhere, bounced twice, then also disappeared from view.

The new hands that grabbed her were ruthlessly strong and professional. Those hands went swiftly under her arms and joined together at the back of her neck, then her head was pulled ruthlessly down to her knees. This was a double Nelson from which she could not break free, however hard she writhed and twisted. So she gave up and went limp, allowing the sweating and cursing uniformed sergeant of the Norfolk Constabulary to drag her through the gap in the hedge to the car-park beyond, and the waiting police van.

'Put the cuffs on this skinny bitch,' he snarled to his equally ruffled colleagues there. 'She's tougher than she looks. Bloody well tossed Taffy Roberts right over the flaming table, she did.'

Brenda said nothing.

In truth she felt breathless and dazed, and now that the euphoria of battle had receded, aches and pains were starting to appear. Her shins had taken some stick from the heels of those boots, and her neck was sore from the sergeant's manhandling, but there were better reasons for maintaining a silence. After all, she was here incognito, and her task of assessing the murderous inclinations of the three Mad Dogs committee members was incomplete. To reveal her true identity in front of these other forlorn and bloodied occupants of the police van into which she had been unceremoniously bundled would ruin her chances of ever doing so, covertly anyway. Besides which, all the members of the Great Yarmouth police that she had seen looked extremely harassed, and it was doubtful whether any of them had time for the quiet tête-à-tête which would be necessary for her to explain her circumstances; even if she were able to get at her identifying warrant card, which was tucked safely away in a zipped breast pocket on the inside of her leather jacket. With her hands cuffed behind her, that was impossible, neither would she willingly invite anyone else to retrieve it. So she settled back to await a more opportune moment. As for the Mad Dogs, for the moment she would have to leave them to Alison.

Whether the fracas had been caused by local or visiting Mods or Rockers, or by unruly elements from the bikers' rally itself, she had no way of telling.

Just as the van doors were slammed closed she saw a distinctly groggy-looking Jim Vine and an anxious-looking Alison Knott come momentarily into view. Then the van was driven away.


The law-enforcers of Great Yarmouth were having one of their busiest nights – since this time last year. There was trouble all over the place: in pubs, fun-fairs, the bus station and the disco halls. It seemed as if all of East Anglia's hooligans had congregated to the one place, at the same time. Most of the off-duty police officers had been called in, and the police station was as crowded as a fog-bound Heathrow.

The system for recording and booking detainees allowed for no short cuts or variations, and the search for drugs and drug-users took extra time. By the time Brenda's van arrived, the main hall of the station was completely congested, so the newcomers had to wait their turn in cells or guarded rooms. A perspiring police doctor naturally gave those who were bloodied or injured precedence over the apparently fit and healthy, and since Brenda was considered one of the latter, she had to wait a long time. Although her handcuffs were taken off, there was little she could do but stretch out her legs and make herself as comfortable as she could, on a hard wooden chair in a corner of a cell. At least she was warm and dry.

Her turn for booking came at just after one o'clock in the morning, when the main hall was nearly empty.

Instead of emptying her pockets as she was instructed, she merely took out her warrant card and laid it carefully on the desk in front of the duty sergeant.

'Your CID have been notified I'm on your patch. I'm on a murder inquiry. Sorry, Taffy,' she said to the bedraggled constable who had fetched her from the cells, 'but you came up behind me. I didn't know you were one of us,' she explained casually, half raising a hand to stifle a yawn.

The duty sergeant raised his eyebrows and stared intently at the clear-eyed, tousle-haired young woman.

'Take her upstairs to the CID room, Taffy,' he said eventually, then he tore the form he'd started writing out into tiny shreds, and dropped them in the waste-paper basket.

'I can have a car take you back to the campsite now, if you like,' the Detective Inspector offered some minutes later, 'but if you want your cover to stay intact, it would be better to spend the rest of the night downstairs in the cells with the others. We'll kick most of them out in the morning, with just a warning, but it's up to you.'

'I'll go back to the cells,' Brenda decided firmly, 'but I'll make the time to have that cup of coffee you promised me first, if you don't mind.'


The weather in North London was cool and overcast.

The scruffily clad driver of the surveillance vehicle, an old builder's van, parked at the appropriate spot in the street where Peter Ellis lived, pulled on the handbrake, got out and locked the doors, then walked away.

In the back of the van, the Enfield police sergeant first made radio contact with his HQ, then slowly wound down the handles that locked the van's rear suspension. When that was done, he and Detective Chief Inspector Sidney Walsh could move about behind the one-way glass windows without the vehicle rocking, and betraying their presence.

Walsh settled himself down in the seat from where he could see the drab row of bay-windowed terraced houses opposite. Number 10 was the one he was interested in. That had a green wooden gate to the short garden, and a black front door surmounted by a round-topped pane of frosted glass. Between the two houses to the right was the narrow gap that led to the passage running behind the back gardens.

The street was well lit, and there was a little activity, but nothing concerning number 10. People came out of other houses, or went in. Cars drew up or drove away. People walked, strolled or slouched along the pavements.

Later, a group of young men came past, kicking at an old tin can. After a few moments one of those young men came back on his own. He looked furtively about him, up and down the street, then headed towards the van. They could see him quite clearly. He reached for the driver's door handle, found it was locked, so he inserted what looked like a simple screwdriver into the keyhole, gave a quick turn, and moments later was in the driver's seat, fumbling beneath the dashboard.

'Christ, this stupid bastard's nicking us,' the sergeant whispered in obvious amazement.

Indeed it was true, for the engine started with a roar and the van shot off down the road so suddenly that the sergeant lost his balance and fell over.

He was soon on his knees, grabbing for the radio's microphone.

'Control! Control! Surveillance vehicle S22 is being stolen,' he announced calmly above the noise of the engine. 'He's slowed right down now. He's no joy-rider. We're turning into Charles Street now, going west. What do you want us to do? Take him ourselves, or find out where he's going?'

Walsh snatched the second pair of earphones, just in time to hear the reply. 'Sit tight. Change to patrol car frequency.'

The sergeant turned a knob, and spoke again. 'We're round the roundabout now, on the A10, heading north.'

It would have been perfectly possible for them to slide back the door to the front cab and force the driver to stop, but obviously the Enfield police had other ideas.

Walsh spoke into his hand radio, his means of contact with Reg, who was sitting in Peter Ellis's garden shed.

'Reg, a slight hiccup with our plans. You're on your own, now. Our van's just been pinched, and we're still in it. We might end up in Scotland. Who knows?'

'Bully for you, boss,' came the faint reply. 'Send us a postcard.'

They didn't get as far as Scotland, though. After a few more twists and turns they drove into a small factory estate, and slowed right down. The van swung sharply to the right, straight into one of the small units, one that had its main door waiting wide open. No sooner had the van come to a stop, than that roller-shutter door was being wound down by one of three burly, thickset men in green dungarees.

The sergeant hurriedly reported their final destination, then took off his earphones.

'I don't like this at all,' he whispered to Walsh. 'Two of them's the Magragh brothers, and they're a right vicious pair. It could be five or ten minutes before help gets here.'

The lights inside the building came on.

Walsh took a quick look round.

'There,' he said softly, pointing to a fire door with a crash bar exit, on the long wall. 'We'll just keep quiet until help comes, but if they find out we're in here, we make a break for that door, keeping together, right?' Odds of two to four were not worth taking – besides, an open door would be useful when help did arrive.

One of the burly men came over as the young driver got out.

'This'll do, all right. Any trouble?' he grunted.

The driver shook his head. 'Engine's all right but the bloody springs 'ave gone on the back. 'Orrible ride, bumps about all over the place. I heard somethin' fall over when I drove away, but I dunno what it was.'

'Let's 'ave a look then. You might 'ave got a few bobs' worth of tools in here. You never know.'

They went round to the back of the van.

Inside, the sergeant freed the internal door catch, then both he and Walsh made themselves ready. Each had a foot placed firmly near the middle of either rear door. As the handle turned and the locking bolts came free from their sockets, they both kicked hard, smashing those doors wide open and straight into the faces of the two men outside. Then they leapt out and ran for the fire door.

Things didn't quite go according to plan, though.

The sergeant, in his haste, stumbled over the driver, and blocked Walsh's way. So Walsh had to turn at bay, as the other two men dashed over. His fists were raised and clenched and a fearsomely aggressive expression appeared on his face. That expression did not deter either of the approaching men, but Walsh's right fist did. It caused one of them to rock right back on his heels as it came crashing into his face. Walsh stepped carefully back, and swung another punch. That missed by a mile, and so did another, but his flailing fists served to keep the fourth man at a distance, and gave time for the sergeant to scramble to his feet and go charging at the fire door, pushing at the crash bar with his hands. Fortunately it opened easily, and it allowed the three uniformed police officers outside to dash in. With three of the four men, if not exactly *hors de combat*, certainly distinctly groggy, it did not take long for the forces of law and order to have them all securely under lock and key.

Another three-quarters of an hour passed before the van could be returned to the street, opposite Peter Ellis's house, to resume its surveillance. Reg Finch was still in position, and apparently A.M. had not yet kept his appointment with the dubiously reformed stolen property fence.

If A.M. was going to do so, he was leaving it a bit late tonight. By now the pubs had closed and their customers were safely home. Any movements stood out against the stillness like a sore thumb. Walsh eased his cramped legs and wriggled into a different position before filling his pipe.

A car turned into the road, and pulled up outside number 14. Walsh tensed expectantly as a tall, well-built girl got out.

'That's Annie Moreton,' the sergeant breathed into Walsh's ear. 'She a tart. She works a patch near Liverpool Street station. Done her bit for the night, obviously. That's her pimp, seeing her home safe and sound, with his share of her takings in his pocket, no doubt.'

Walsh settled back, as comfortably as he could. He ought to be used to these vigils – he'd done enough in his time. Tonight's, though, had been more active than most. His right hand felt sore from its contact with that thug's face, but he felt quite pleased with the way he'd reacted when faced by opponents both younger and fitter than he. There was life in the old boy yet. The surveillance van had been stolen for use in a raid on a Securicor truck, so the Enfield men had reckoned, but Walsh hadn't been all that interested. It was a murderer that he was after. In another hour they could pack up and go home, but the problem would remain, for if A.M. did not come tonight, perhaps he had been unavoidably delayed. Maybe he'd come tomorrow night instead. That would mean another watch would have to be organised, but a decision on that could wait until morning.

Arthur Bryant had made himself as comfortable as he could. He'd brought a sleeping bag with him when he'd relieved the previous watcher of the excavation site, at ten thirty last night. He'd crept into the dry dead leaves under a large rhododendron that was just readying itself for its annual glorious burst into masses of purple flowers. There he had a good wide field of vision that encompassed trench 'K', the target area, and all its approaches, albeit considerably foreshortened by being so near ground level. He found that lying flat on his stomach meant that he needed to prop himself up on his elbows and crane his neck back, a position which became very tiring after only a short time. So he wriggled out of his sleeping bag and moved from under the rhododendron to a position further along the wood, where he could sit with his back against the rough trunk of a giant Scots pine.

At about two o'clock in the morning he spotted movement at the edge of the wood on the far side of the open area – a low, rounded, huddled shape, which to his tired eyes, even through his light-intensifier binoculars, took the form of a man crawling Indian-fashion. He was reaching for his radio to give warning and summon assistance when the shape came further out into the open, and he saw the white cross stripes of a badger.

It took years for a grey overcast dawn to come and ease away the blackness of night. Then he returned to the rhododendron, and discarded the binoculars. At eight thirty, when his relief arrived, he could cautiously roll up his sleeping bag, collect his gear, and slink away to the main road, where a panda car would pick him up, and take him home.

# 10

The surveillance of the house in North London was undertaken again the following night.

As do those watch-keeping officers of a lonely ship in an empty ocean, those involved maintained their professional vigilance, in spite of the feeling that theirs would be a fruitless task, and that they would see nothing of interest. Duty, training and determination made them ready to play the few cards they had been dealt to their maximum effect, but in this case that effect was zero.

Arthur Bryant spent his second night sitting with his back to the tall Scots pine at the edge of the wood in Hinching Park. No one visited that excavation site during the hours of darkness, but he did have the dubious pleasure of seeing two badgers out on their nocturnal ventures this time.

Detective Constable Alison Knott had spent much of the previous night on fruitless visits to the Great Yarmouth police station, hoping to secure Brenda's early release. So the following night, in her warm sleeping-bag, sleep came quickly and easily, long before the last returning motor bike had puttered carefully across the uneven surface of the field. A little after that there came the light patter of rain on the tent, announcing the arrival overhead of some of those black clouds that had been building up over the silvery grey sea to the east.

Brenda Phipps, however, lay in the limbo state that an over-tired mind sometimes has to pass through before it can sink into genuine sleep. Her subconscious recognised the sounds of the last returning motor bike and accepted them as normal and harmless, but the first light pats of rain on to the taut material of the tent sounded like someone outside tapping to attract attention. That possibility made her mind come instantly wide awake, then, having identified the true cause of those sounds, she found that sleep had been driven far away. Her thoughts began a replay of recent events. That young constable she'd tossed over her shoulder last night had obviously been very impressed at coming up against an incognito plain-clothed officer sleuthing a murder investigation. Even that Detective Inspector had clearly shown his approval of her determination to carry on with her covert inquiries.

It had all worked out very much in her favour, in the end. Her arrival back at the campsite, after her release, had had all the hallmarks of the return of the conquering heroine.

Apparently the story of her standing over the senseless form of Jim Vine, like some Valkyrie from Valhalla, and taking on all comers, law and order included, had spread rapidly, for pretty well the whole of the camp had turned out to greet and cheer her return.

It had been quite embarrassing, really.

She'd been made an honorary member of no fewer than a dozen different motor-cycle clubs, and now had their badges pinned to the front of her leather jacket, like a row of military medals.

Ironically, the blaze of publicity given to an incognito undercover agent had had an unexpected bonus: it had allowed her to circulate the camp, once she'd shaken Jim Vine off from following her around like a love-lorn sheep. She'd had a ready welcome at any group, with the conversation topic almost pre-set to the Mad Dog club, which was just what she'd wanted.

'Inseparable, them three,' someone had told her, referring to Jim and the other two committee members. 'Real Three Musketeers. Went to school together, been great pals ever since, and still do things together, even though they've now got wives and kids, or two of them have.'

That had rather taken her aback. Somehow the picture in her mind of the three of them together, beating the life out of Sir Gordon Lignum, did not seem at all right. One of them on his own, maybe – but the Three Musketeers together? That seemed wrong.

The girl, Samantha Leverington, didn't seem generally well known; her accident had not been common knowledge outside her local club, nor did it excite anything more than offhanded sympathy. What was universal, though, was the vitriolic reaction to the 'I didn't see you' brigade, and the inadequate sentences given as punishment.

'Eighty-one pounds, that was all the driver got fined, and the poor sod who got knocked off his bike spent four months in hospital. He's now registered disabled and lucky not to have lost his leg altogether. It's ridiculous. A car's like a hand-grenade – bloody dangerous if you fool about with it.' These were the sort of stories she'd heard, and the sentiments that had been expressed so strongly.

The patter of rain had stopped and almost absent-mindedly Brenda wriggled out of her sleeping-bag and began to pull on her leather gear. With her mind as active as it was now, and her body so tense and restless, sleep was not going to be forthcoming, not soon anyway. She needed fresh air and exercise.

At home in her flat, if such a set of circumstances occurred, there was a ready solution to hand – she would do some work on one of her chipped or broken pieces of porcelain. That demanded such a degree of concentration that even after a very short period all extraneous thoughts were soon washed clear from her mind.

It was a little three-inch bowl that was testing her patience at the moment. She hadn't been able to resist buying that piece of Wedgwood 'fairy lustre', in spite of its damage, not once she'd picked it up and held it in her hands. Such a piece had never come her way before. It had been broken into three parts and crudely glued together. Even so, it had cost her more than she'd wanted to pay. That woman at the car-boot sale had been shrewd enough to recognise the enthusiasm that her prospective customer was desperately trying to hide, and had stuck doggedly to her ridiculously high price, until Brenda's bargaining resources had disintegrated. Restoration, though, posed problems she'd not before encountered. Her expertise with vibrant Coalport or Meissen colours was of little use with these subtle shades and their elusive lustre. Still, patience, trial and error, a little luck and a judicious use of acid, were gradually bringing success, but it would take a lot of time to achieve the perfection she strove for.

She set off, wandering towards the dunes and the beach.

The occasional light from a half-moon through the patchy cloud was enough to enable her to avoid the guy-ropes of tents, and the parked motor cycles, without breaking the train of her thoughts.

A petition had been organised by the Bikers' Federation, a few years previously, asking the government to look into the prevalence of 'I didn't see you' accidents involving motor cyclists. Possibly that had resulted in the television adverts exhorting drivers of cars to watch out with greater care. She'd heard nothing to indicate other organised action, either legal or illegal, but the depths of feeling expressed were so strong that spasmodic isolated vigilante action was very possible.

Brenda picked her way carefully along the path of old railway sleepers that led through the dunes. Before her was the wide expanse of beach exposed by the ebbing tide. The flickering and changing lines of luminescent white from the breaking rippling waves seemed a long way away.

Faint alien sounds penetrated her thoughts. She stopped still to listen.

Someone was negotiating the path back there, and had probably stumbled in the gaps between the wooden sleepers.

Was that somebody following her? If so, then those sounds were the first she'd heard.

She felt no fear; her confidence in her ability to look after herself was quite complete. If some male had seen her walking through the camp unaccompanied and fancied his chances at molesting a lone helpless woman, then he'd be in for a hell of a shock. One that would do his ego no good at all.

She ran quickly from the beach into a gap in the dunes and stood there in the shadows, waiting and watching.

It was some moments before the figure arrived. It was a male. He halted as he glanced up and down the beach looking for his quarry; not seeing her, he climbed to the top of the nearest dune to give himself a better view. There was something about his posture – the slightly rounded shoulders, the way he held his head – that identified him as Jim Vine.

For a moment Brenda considered calling out and confronting him, but she quickly cast that idea aside. She wanted no company, and certainly not that of a tongue-tied man who would leave all the talking to her. So she ducked down low, and waited. Vine would surely go along the beach one way or the other, looking for her. After five long minutes, satisfied that he'd gone the wrong way, she stood up again and returned to the path by climbing the side of the soft sand dune, then set off to walk back to the campsite.

She now felt physically tired, but far more important, during those moments in the dunes she had come to a decision. She and Alison might spend hours and hours talking about the possibility that one of these motor-cycle characters might have exacted a violent vengeance on a negligent motorist, but they would still not be able to advance the investigation into the murder of Sir Gordon Lignum in any way.

Brenda's brain had come up with a possible solution to the problem; having done that, all her mind now wanted to do was to switch off and rest, and that it did, the moment she'd got herself back in her sleeping-bag.

# 11

'You've done what, Brenda?' Walsh said, leaning forward with his elbows on his desk and frowning deeply as he stared intently at her.

'I did what I thought was best, Chief,' Brenda explained. 'Maybe it'll help resolve this bikers' angle, or maybe it won't, but at least we'll have tried.'

'Let me get this clear,' Walsh said slowly. 'You've had Alison's brother make out that you and he had a motor-bike accident on the way back from your rally –'

'That's right,' Brenda interrupted impatiently. 'The story is that Alison's brother had no injuries, but I've broken my arm and suffered a lot of pain. We've said that I've not been detained in hospital, otherwise they might want to visit me there. As it is, they can't, and they don't know where I live.'

'And you've raked in poor old Arthur Bryant to play the "I didn't see you" car driver,' Reg Finch added with a rather supercilious grin.

'That's right. Alison's brother has already phoned the chairman of the Mad Dogs, and told him all about it, including where Arthur lives. If those three are dishing out punishment when anyone they happen to fancy gets hurt, then Arthur will get a visit, and we'll catch them red-handed. It's quite simple, isn't it? If that does happen then the chances are that we'll have caught Lignum's killers.' Brenda glared challengingly back at Walsh.

Sidney Walsh scratched aimlessly at the side of his head. He felt a reluctance to approve of Brenda's scheme, possibly because it had been arranged without his prior knowledge, but it also meant manning yet another surveillance exercise. He had been intending to carry on the observation of the North London house for one more night, hoping the unknown A.M. might still turn up to try and collect some reward for his ill-gotten loot.

Brenda's action meant that for the next few days all his team were going to be wasting a lot of time just watching and waiting, deadening their minds and dulling intellects that needed to be wide awake and alert. Paperwork, and other lines of investigation on this and other cases, would be delayed.

He felt an urge to blindly lose his temper, but one of the prime qualities he'd looked for in selecting his team members was their ability to think and act for themselves, so he could hardly complain when one of them did just that. He needed to support them and encourage them, not to nullify and stultify their initative.

They were both watching him keenly. Could they sense the thoughts in his mind?

He shrugged his shoulders phlegmatically, smiled ruefully, and merely said, 'It looks as though we're all going to be pretty busy for the next few days, then.'

Was that relief expressed in their eyes? You'd have thought they'd known him better. Never mind, it was time to get on with other things. He'd best make sure that what time could be devoted to more methodical investigations was used to its best advantage.

'Did you enjoy your night in the cells, Brenda?' Reg asked with a grin.

'Not a lot. You had a bit of fun too, I gather, Chief,' Brenda responded brightly.

'You could say that. Unexpected, certainly. Now, Ingrid Lignum's alibi is still standing up, is it, Brenda?' Walsh asked, determined to keep the conversation on the matter in hand.

'Yes, Chief. I think that if Ingrid Lignum is involved in her husband's murder, then we've got to be looking for an accomplice. It can't be the schoolteacher choirmaster, but it could be that solicitor, David Grant, if we could break his alibi at the golf club.'

'Or someone from her shady past,' Reg suggested.

'Possibly. No, I might be wrong, but if she latched on to Sir Gordon as a step up the social ladder then I wouldn't put it past her to dump him if someone else came into her orbit offering better prospects. She's an attractive woman, with plenty of experience in making herself desirable.'

'I can see that,' Walsh mused with a frown of concentration, 'but better prospects for what? A higher social position and more wealth? I can't see anyone with those qualities being an accomplice in violent murder, just to achieve an objective that could be attained by a simple divorce.'

'He might have become so besotted with her that common sense no longer played a part,' Brenda suggested.

'In that case, boss, he shouldn't be difficult to find,' Reg said confidently. 'If he's rich, with a high social standing and a bit stupid where women are concerned, how about a senior military officer or a government minister? One of those should fit the bill.'

'Do be sensible, Reg,' Brenda snapped irritably.

'He's right, though,' Walsh said, shaking his head. 'Not necessarily about officers or government ministers, but if someone like that has come within her social orbit recently, you might find a potential accomplice. We've checked the Polytechnic and the charities, so it must be someone she'd met through Lignum's University contacts. Find out Lignum's social engagements during the past few months, Brenda, and their guest lists, then go and interview some of them – the women especially. They always notice what other women are up to, and they'd spot a besotted man a mile off.'

Brenda nodded. 'All right, but if we want to find social gossip like that I might just as well cut the corners and ask Professor Hughes for advice. He usually knows who's who and what's what.'

'Right! Now what's going on at the excavation site, Reg? Are they down to the level where the tablet was found yet?'

'Not yet,' Reg replied. 'They're digging a pretty wide swath on either side of the original trench, but they're doing it properly and carefully, so they've a few feet more to clear before they get down to the critical level. Choosely's been ill with a tummy bug for the last couple of days, and since he won't let them work on it unless he's there, they haven't got very far. Give them a few more days yet, and then it'll get critical.'

'Do we really need someone watching tonight, then?' Walsh asked hopefully.

Reg nodded. 'I'm afraid so, boss. An hour's vigorous work with a spade would effectively destroy the site.'

Walsh reached for his pipe, and started to fill it slowly. 'Reg, put your boot to Choosely's backside, will you? The sooner that site's cleared, the sooner we can cut out one of our surveillance operations. Brenda, you'll have to be with Arthur this evening in case your motor-bike thugs turn up. At least they won't beat him up too badly if you show your face. We'd better find you a uniformed chap as back-up. You'll only need to be there until eleven or so, won't you? They won't come later than that. So if Alison does the first watch on the archaeological site, Arthur can take over from her when you finish at his place,' Walsh decided firmly. 'We'll have to organise things differently tomorrow evening. It's the Beethoven's Ninth concert, and we've got to be there or we'll have the C.C.'s wife breathing down our necks. I don't know which would be worse, him or her.'

Reg's face showed signs of anguish. 'I must be there, boss. My name'll be mud if I don't turn up.'

Walsh looked serious. Obviously Reg's private life had suffered during the past few days of late-night operations, as indeed had his own. Duty may be duty but their married lives needed to be protected too. Even understanding wives could be pushed too far.

'You'll be all right, Reg. We'll make tonight's Enfield watch the last. We've wasted enough time there as it is,' Walsh promised. 'Now, our two prime suspects, MacGregor and Fairbrother. We've left them alone for a few days now, so maybe their nerves will be starting to play up. It's time we had another go at them. I did the first interviews with Brenda, so you and Alison can do them tomorrow, Reg. I'd better get off now. I've arranged to meet Lignum's next of kin – the tenth baronet. He arrived here last night from New Zealand.'

'Yes, Professor Hughes did ring me earlier to say that you might call.' The plump woman's chubbily attractive face smiled pleasantly, but her eyes were shrewd and observant as she assessed and summed up her visitor.

'What a cheek that man's got! He said that among the historico-archaeological fraternity I was the biggest gossip he knew, and that he wanted me to tell you all the scandal. So I put him straight in his place. "No woman can be a member of a fraternity, Edwin," I said. "Besides, when it comes to gossiping, you leave me standing any day of the week." He's a lovely chap, Edwin, and he's got a great sense of humour, but I knew he was being serious when he also said I was a woman in a million – a gossip who could keep her mouth shut. Now, I do take that as a compliment. So you want to ask me about Ingrid Lignum do you?'

Brenda Phipps leaned back in the chintz-covered easy chair, and nodded. There didn't seem a lot of point in opening her mouth to speak, since the chances of her being able to utter more than a few words were slim.

'Well, you know,' the gossip went on cheerfully, 'if you want to hear scandal about her and other men, or about Gordon and other women, then I'm afraid you're going to be disappointed. I've been racking my brain ever since Edwin phoned, and I can't think of anything juicy about either of them. Mind you, it opened a few eyes pretty wide when he suddenly turned up with her on his arm. Everyone thought poor old Gordon was going to end up with that weird skinny Edwina woman from Animal Husbandry, the one who does the AID research. That would have livened him up a bit, if she did to him what she likes doing to those bulls they've got there. It's funny what turns some people on. I wouldn't fancy doing it myself. No, it came as a shock when Gordon suddenly turned up with his curvy blonde Swede. No one thought it would last. There were plenty of fellows in the early days who fancied their chances, and now I come to think of it, there were plenty like me watching to see what would happen. Very deftly handled, they were. Without causing a scene, or any acrimony that I can remember, she put them firmly in their place. I remember thinking at the time that she knew a bit more about men than anyone gave her credit for. After a while, since nothing juicy happened, people gave up watching particularly. I know I did. Gordon seemed very happy, to me, and she seemed contented enough. There must have been more in poor Gordon than we ever thought there was,' she added regretfully, 'and we'll never know about it now, will we?'

Mrs Choosely was a tall, thin woman with dark hair and tense frowning facial features.

'Come in, Sergeant. Charles is working in his study. He oughtn't to be, he should be in bed. You mind you don't catch it from him. It's a tummy bug they say is going round. The boys brought it home from school. I've only just got over it myself, and it really pulls you down. They say it's a bug, but it's more likely nitrates or some such chemicals got in the water.'

It wasn't archaeological work that was occupying the pale-faced, dressing-gowned Charles Choosely in the tiny room partitioned off from the back of the garage, for the small desk top contained cheque book, bank statements, and a pile of bills. Those were all hastily swept into a drawer, but before they disappeared Reg did manage to glimpse a whole row of O/Ds next to the right-hand column on the top bank statement.

'We're anxious to get this trench "K" business finalised,' Reg explained.

'And so am I,' Choosely acknowledged.

'How soon can you get back on to it, then, and how long will it take, do you think?'

'I'm a lot better today than I was yesterday, so hopefully I'll be all right tomorrow. There's still another foot or so to go before we get to the critical level. We should be down to that the day after tomorrow. If not then, certainly the next day. I've asked Mildren from Jesus and Sorenson from Trinity to be there as well, and Hughes from Downing wants to come. I can't see any of them being keen to get on their knees with a trowel, but they'll be independent witnesses if anything interesting does turn up. Not that I'm expecting it will, mind you. With you and your forensic lot as well, there'll be quite a crowd, so I've arranged for a catering firm to bring out a hamper lunch, with some wine and so on. You might think that's being a bit extravagant,' he said, looking a trifle sheepish. 'We don't normally have such luxuries, but I had a chap come up from London the other day, from the people who are planning to develop the site, you know, and he gave me five hundred pounds to spend on refreshments for the students. If I needed more, I'd only got to ask. Wasn't that thoughtful of him?'

125

Sir Adrian Lignum was obviously not yet used to his new title, for he reddened in embarrassment when Walsh used it.

He was about average height, that is to say five feet ten-ish, reasonably good-looking, a bit podgy round the waist, and in his middle twenties. He had dark hair neatly trimmed round the back of his neck, and his face was pale and drawn, with a nervous tic twitching spasmodically beneath his left eye. Possibly he was suffering from jetlag after the long flight from his native land.

'Gordon's father was my uncle,' Sir Adrian explained rather tentatively.

'You're a solicitor with a legal firm in Wellington, I understand,' Walsh said.

'That's right. Mind you, I've been offered an actual partnership now.'

'Did you know your cousin well?' Walsh asked.

'We'd never met. This is the first time I've been abroad, as a matter of fact. I'd have come over sooner, only it took some time to get myself a passport. We did write to each other occasionally, Christmas cards and so on, but, well, you know how it is. The family wasn't close, and I never dreamt I'd ever come into the title. I still can't quite believe it.'

'So, you can't tell me much about him then?' Walsh's voice sounded a little despondent. It was beginning to look as though he would learn little from this interview to help his investigations.

'I doubt it. He got married a few years ago. My mother was still alive then, but she wasn't well and I couldn't leave her, so I never came over, though I was invited of course. I was planning to go and see his wife this afternoon, and I've got to see this fellow Grant about the trust some time, but to tell the truth, I still feel a bit queasy, so I might put that off for today. It's being stuck in a Boeing 747 for all that time, I suppose, and all the hassle at both ends. Lord, I've never seen anything like your London airport. If travelling means fighting your way through places like that, I think I'd rather stay back home in Wellington. England's very nice, I'm sure, but it's so crowded, isn't it? Do you know when the funeral will be? I don't know anyone over here, but I must stay for that. It wouldn't look right if I didn't, would it?'

# 12

'You are an untidy beggar, Arthur,' Brenda Phipps pronounced, having swept a critical glance round the sitting-room of Detective Constable Arthur Bryant's bachelor flat. 'This place is like a pigsty. It hasn't been vacuumed or seen a duster for weeks – and don't you ever empty that thing?' she went on, pointing to the waste-paper basket in the corner, which had overflowed with old newspapers and crisp packets. 'And it whiffs in here. It's like Billingsgate market on a hot Monday morning. Open a window, for heaven's sake. Let some fresh air in, do.'

Arthur scowled. 'What chance have I had to do housework lately?' he protested as he pushed open one of the casement windows. 'I've hardly been here, except to eat and sleep, and I haven't had much time to do those either. If the Chief Inspector keeps this pressure up much longer, I can see us all ending up in the loony bin . . .'

'You'd qualify as it is, Arthur, but I don't know why you're moaning. A young healthy fellow like you shouldn't grumble about having to do a bit of hard work. Anyway, all you've had to do is sit quietly for a few hours, and do a bit of watching. You're getting plenty of fresh air, and you can't say you're not seeing a bit of the night life, can you?'

Arthur shrugged his shoulders phlegmatically, and went over to close the door to the bedroom. He didn't want Brenda nosing about in there, not the way things were.

'That's the only thing on the plus side,' he muttered, 'the night life, I mean. There's a badger set round there somewhere, just inside the woods. About midnight they come out into the open and go nosing about feeding. When dawn breaks all the birds start up too. I like that. There's loads of jays, squirrels and rabbits as well.'

'See, you're having a whale of a time out there,' Brenda went on. 'Now, do I get offered a cup of coffee, or am I expected to make it myself?'

'I'll make it,' Arthur said, hastily heading for his tiny kitchen. There was time, while the kettle was coming to the boil, to nip into the bathroom, put out two clean towels, and scrub away the grime in the wash-basin with the nail brush. There would be little his visitor could nag about in there, or in the kitchen for that matter, not when he'd slipped the unwashed crockery out of sight into the cupboard under the sink.

In the sitting-room Brenda had finished perusing the titles of the tapes and CDs under the music centre and the numerous books in the bookcase. In spite of her teasing, she was not unimpressed with Arthur's style of living. The furniture was sensible and comfortable. It had been expensive once, for it was obviously not new, and the books and tapes showed a nice blend of the classic and the popular. As Arthur came back in with coffee cups on a neat wooden tray, she turned her attention to a small glass-fronted display cabinet, on the shelves of which were set out a number of stylistic, solid-looking, glass animals and birds. Some were plain clear glass, others had specks of colour encased within.

'You need more light to display them properly,' Brenda advised, 'and you shouldn't use that kind of wire spring hanger on that plate on the wall over there, it'll damage the rim, you know, and spoil it, but I do like that little bowl you've got on the television. That's Imari, about sixty or seventy years old, I'd say.'

'That was my great-aunt's. Is your coffee all right? Would you like more milk?' he asked.

'No thanks. It's fine.'

'Do you really think these motor-cycle chaps'll come?'

Brenda shrugged her slim shoulders. 'I don't know. I hope so. Now, food. We've got to eat, we won't get much chance later. I'm your guest. What have you got?'

Arthur's face took on a startled look, yet he could not prevent the hint of a grin appearing at the corner of his mouth. 'I can do you a fried egg, or beans on toast. Whichever you prefer.'

Brenda scowled at him suspiciously, and took herself off into the kitchen. Arthur's face was all grin as he heard the fridge door being opened.

'We'll have the seafood platter,' she called out. 'I'll put it in the microwave, you can lay the table and –' She was interrupted by the ringing of the front door bell.

She came back into the sitting-room, looking thoughtfully serious. 'If it's them, be careful, Arthur. If it looks like trouble, back off. Let them follow you in here, then I'll come out and confront them.'

Arthur licked his lips, pulled back his shoulders, and went to open the door.

'Is your name Bryant? Arthur Bryant?' demanded the shorter of the two neatly suited and respectably dressed men.

'Yes, it is,' Arthur replied, a little disappointedly. He'd steeled himself up, expecting to find three big threatening leather-clad motor bikers. Instead, here were two men who looked like law-upholders, not law-breakers, but possibly they were the solicitor and the accountant Brenda had talked about, so he set himself to play his part.

'If you're selling life insurance,' he went on, 'or double glazing, I'm not in the market, I'm afraid.'

'Neither of those, but you might call us health visitors, for it's your health we're concerned about. May we come in?' the taller man asked drily.

Arthur frowned. Perhaps he was wrong and these two were prepared for physical violence – their voices had a threatening tone. He shook his head. 'Whatever it is you're selling, I'm not interested, thank you. I've not the time anyway, I'm expecting visitors.' He started to close the door, but he'd hardly moved it an inch before the shorter one had stepped boldly forward into the doorway.

'I really do think it would be wise for you to listen to what we have to say, Mr Bryant,' he said.

This was more like what he'd expected, so Arthur took a step back. The visitor promptly moved forward again, and Arthur found himself being ushered back into his own sitting-room. He looked round quickly, expecting Brenda to be there to take control of the situation, but there was no sign of her. He cleared his throat nervously.

'Well, now you're in, you might as well say your piece. What do you want?'

'Yesterday, Mr Bryant, you were out in your car, and you were involved in an accident. Correct?'

Arthur's eyes narrowed suspiciously. 'So? What if I was?'

'That accident involved a motor cycle, and the pillion rider sustained serious injury.'

Arthur shrugged his shoulders in a gesture of complacency.

'So what? It was his fault. He must have been going at a hell of a lick, much too fast, else I'd have seen him.'

'You didn't see him, Mr Bryant,' the taller man said menacingly, 'because you were being careless and driving without due care and consideration for others on the road. As a result, your lack of attention caused an accident which could easily have proved fatal. Not for you, unfortunately, safe in the steel box of your car, but for the riders on the motor cycle.'

Arthur schooled his facial features into what he thought to be a yobbish grin. He felt confident now that the solicitor and the accountant would never risk their professional reputations by indulging in unseemly brawls – and even if he were wrong, it wasn't a question of two against one, not with Brenda handy in the kitchen, or was she in his untidy bedroom? It seemed likely. That door had been closed, now it was slightly ajar. He would be more provocative with these two, and see what happened.

'That's their problem. Everyone knows motor bikes are dangerous. No one forces them to ride one. Why can't they drive cars like everyone else? If they'd been in a car I'd have seen them. I'm sure I would. In any case, what the hell's it got to do with you? I've given my side of the story to the police,' he went on, speaking more quickly and raising his voice as though he were getting increasingly angry. 'What they do is up to them. So you two can go to hell and get stuffed. You can both –'

'Calm down, Mr Bryant, calm down. There's no point in losing your temper. Let me explain,' the shorter visitor said seriously. 'The girl on the motor bike, the one who was injured, is a friend of ours – and, more importantly, is also a particular friend of a friend. Now this friend is a nice chap, most of the time, but when he gets worked up and angry, he can become . . . how can I put it? Well, sort of violent, and at the moment, he's angry with you, Mr Bryant, because of what you did to his friend. We're here as mediators – peacemakers if you like. If we can find some extenuating circumstances to account for your lamentably careless lack of attention while driving your car, and some signs of due contrition on your part for what happened, then we might be able to calm his anger. He's a kind and understanding man normally, you see, but if we can't do that, there is the distinct possibility that you might meet with, um, physical violence.'

Arthur leaned back in his chair and looked thoughtful. 'I can look after myself,' he muttered.

'That's good, because unless you co-operate, you may well need to.'

'How do you know what your crazy friend will do? Has this sort of thing happened before, then?' Arthur probed cautiously.

There were a few moments' silence that was eventually broken by the taller visitor, speaking very quietly.

'Our friend is not crazy, Mr Bryant. How would you feel if you were the rider of a motor cycle involved in an accident such as yours, and when you got to your feet you found your pillion passenger, your wife of only six months, lying sprawled on the cold road, dead, with a broken neck? How would you feel, Mr Bryant, if the driver of the car just turns round and says, "Sorry, mate, I didn't see you," when it's a clear day and a straight open road? Would you feel angry? Would you want to reach out your hands to that person's throat and choke out of him all the anger and misery you

131

felt at the needless killing of someone you loved? Would you?'

Arthur looked shocked and remained silent.

The answer came from behind the two visitors.

'So that's what happened to Jim Vine, is it?' Brenda said, her voice cool and low-pitched, as she came out of the bedroom. 'What a pity you both didn't get to the man who caused Samantha Leverington's accident before Jim Vine did. You might have been able to prevent a murder if you had.'

The two intruders had risen to their feet, visibly shaken by Brenda's sudden appearance.

'Hello, Graham.' She nodded to the shorter of the two, the solicitor, then to the other, the accountant. 'Hello, Giles. You've rather dropped poor old Jim right in the mire, haven't you?'

Graham found his voice first. 'Your arm? We understood you'd broken your arm. What's going on? What are you doing here, Brenda?'

'She's Detective Constable Brenda Phipps, Cambridgeshire CID, serious crime squad,' Arthur announced dramatically. 'I'm a Detective Constable too. There was no motor cycle accident.'

'So all this is a set-up?' Graham asked, his face reddening angrily.

'A *ruse de guerre*,' Arthur suggested helpfully.

'We're investigating the murder of the man who put Samantha Leverington into hospital,' Brenda announced firmly. 'We know a motor cyclist had been in the room where the crime was committed. It was Jim Vine, was it? I gather he'd taken a shine to Samantha. Right, we'll have him brought in for questioning, then Forensic can go through all his gear and clothing. If they can find anything to tie him down to the scene of the crime, we'll have found our murderer. It was a particularly vicious and cold-blooded killing, and neither the judge nor the jury will have any mercy on him. Jim Vine will go down for life, and I mean life.' She directed the latter part of her prophecy to Giles. He was visibly shocked and clearly appalled by what he'd heard. He opened his mouth to speak, but the cold-eyed solicitor forestalled him.

'Keep your mouth shut, Gil, for God's sake. This is a murder inquiry, don't say anything.'

A frown appeared on Giles's face. 'I don't care if it is a murder inquiry, Graham. We can't let Jim take the can. Christ, you know him. He'll crack up completely if he's put in a cell and questioned for hours on end. It's not right and I won't have it.'

His friend Graham looked mulishly stubborn, and for a moment Brenda thought he was going to remain that way, but eventually he shook his head and smiled ruefully.

'All right, have it your way. The truth will out, they say. Well, Detective Constable Phipps, Jim Vine never went to that house in Newnham. We did! And that man Lignum was alive and well when we left.'

Brenda's eyes narrowed suspiciously. For a moment she had felt very pleased with herself. Her scheming and planning had seemed successful. With Jim Vine as the killer, all was explained neatly and simply. Now these two, instead of confirming it, were casting up new doubts and confusion.

'You three left the hospital that Sunday night together. Why should we believe Jim Vine didn't go with you?' she demanded.

'For the same reason that Jim didn't come here tonight. Jim's no fool, he knows how much he hates the "I didn't see you" brigade. We're his friends, he trusts us. We went to find out if there were any extenuating circumstances, because if there were, then we could tell him and Jim's anger would quickly dissipate,' Graham explained.

'So! What did Sir Gordon Lignum have to say?' Arthur asked.

'He huffed and puffed at first, like you were doing earlier, but when we told him what had happened to Jim Vine's wife, the poor sod nearly burst into tears. He even wanted to give us money, for the club's charitable funds, but we couldn't have that, of course.'

'What else did he have to say?' Brenda prompted.

'He asked us about our club. What it was called, what sort of things we did,' Graham replied.

'The Mad Dogs is an appropriate title, I think,' Brenda mused, partly to herself.

'That's not our official name,' Giles interposed. 'We wanted to call ourselves that, but it was already being used by another club, so we called ourselves the Canines instead.'

'Did Lignum offer any extenuating circumstances, then?' Arthur wanted to know.

'He did indeed. He told us he'd got a tumour, and that it was being tested for malignancy at the time of the accident. Quite understandably, that was worrying him, but to his great relief he'd since learned it was benign, and not malignant.'

Arthur's eyes had suddenly lit up. 'They were there, Brenda,' he said excitedly. 'Those letters and numbers Lignum had written on his pad, "K9" and "B9", they aren't "K9" and "B9" at all, they're "Canine" and "Benign".'

Brenda looked thoughtful. 'Maybe so. Right, where did you park your motor bikes while you were talking to Lignum? Did you see anyone hanging around when you went in, or came out? Did you see any other vehicles nearby? Was he in fact alone in the house? Arthur, have you got some statement forms? We'd better make this official, now.'

'Steady on, Brenda,' Graham the solicitor said. 'Let's take these questions one at a time. We'll do our best to give you answers.'

Walsh was ensconced in the Enfield surveillance van when Brenda rang him on his radio phone to tell him the story of all that had happened in Arthur Bryant's flat.

'Well done. I'm glad it worked out all right,' he replied thoughtfully, 'but if our murderer doesn't turn up down here tonight, and I'm beginning to think he won't, then tomorrow morning you and I ought to have a chat with this Jim Vine. Pick me up from my house at about ten. With a bit of luck I might be awake by then.'

134

# 13

It was a lovely morning for a stroll, or so thought Police Constable Alison Knott as she walked along St Andrew's Street with the tall Sergeant Reg Finch by her side. He'd matched his stride to hers in a nice easy leisurely pace, for they were in no great hurry.

To all these other pedestrians they probably seemed like an ordinary married couple, out to do some shopping in the busy city centre, rather than two serious police officers on a murder inquiry.

That was an amusing thought – marriage to Reg. She liked him, of course, he'd got such nice eyes and long sensitive fingers, and there was no doubt that he'd make a very nice husband, if he were not already someone else's.

When one worked in close proximity with the opposite sex it was difficult sometimes not to wonder how one would react if anything happened to put that relationship on to a more physical level.

It wouldn't be all that difficult in her case, not if Reg wanted to. One look at her with those big blue eyes of his, and she'd be bound to go all limp and gooey.

Her day-dreaming came to an abrupt end as Reg suddenly grabbed her arm and jerked her to a stop.

Back in the world of reality she found a dozen or so undergraduate cyclists just in front of her, forcing their way imperiously through the crowd of pedestrians on the pavement outside the entrance to Emmanuel College.

'I was lost in thought, I'm afraid,' she excused herself with a laugh.

'That's not difficult, when you're on a case like this,' Reg replied in a serious voice. 'The boss thinks he's on a winner with this Jim Vine, but I'm not so sure.'

'Brenda's going with him, isn't she? I don't think she'll enjoy that. I have the feeling she rather likes Jim Vine,' Alison said casually, turning her head so that she could look at Reg's face.

The suggestion that Brenda might have any such feelings seemed to surprise him, for a frown came upon his forehead. It was some moments before he replied, and then he did so with an offhanded shrug of his shoulders.

'Even if she does, I can't see her letting that affect her judgement,' he observed confidently.

Alison felt a twinge of annoyance at this casual dismissal of human feelings. Men seemed to make such a fetish about controlling and concealing emotions, as though that were a laudable quality in itself. Reg was certainly not the cold hard man he tried to portray. There was his involvement with the orphanage, for instance, his liking for dogs, and his sense of humour. She gave an inaudible sigh. Reg was right to keep his emotions firmly under control. She must do the same, but nevertheless, what went on inside her own mind was her own business.

When they came to the Round Church they turned right, down the narrow lane which led to the small maze of streets containing the rows of tall houses in which Melissa Fairbrother had her bed-sit.


Melissa's natural jauntiness and liveliness of manner were not so evident today. She'd had plenty of mental resilience to tide her over the initial shock of suddenly finding herself entangled in the unthinkably horrific tentacles of a murder inquiry, but that strength had gradually weakened as the days had passed by. It had slowly dawned on her that her instinctive belief in the natural infallibility of British justice, bolstered as it was by a righteous upbringing and a fair dose of Sherlock Holmes and Perry Mason, was somewhat naïve. A few days ago life had seemed a glorious thing, full of brightness and excitement; now it oozed with a corrupting mixture of depression, hopelessness and fear.

136

Perhaps it was not surprising that Melissa wore black jeans and a black T-shirt this morning.

She sat on the divan in her room, leaning back on the brightly coloured cushions, with her knees pulled up protectively to her chin and held there by tightly clasped hands.

Reg Finch studied the girl's face intently. He took his time over it, and made no effort to hide what he was doing. The silence and accusing stare were potent stress-raising weapons in an interview of this type. She made no attempt to stare him down, but turned her glance away. The signs of strain on her face were quite apparent. There was a puffiness round the eyes that suggested lack of sleep, and the eyes themselves were dull. The poor girl was dreadfully unhappy, Reg thought, but he forced himself to view her without sympathy. It was not too difficult to do that if he reminded himself that possibly she was a murderer, or the accomplice of one.

'You said in your earlier statement that you and MacGregor had not been close friends before the incident with the cuneiform tablet, and that it was only afterwards that he started to pay particular attention to you. Why do you think he did that?' Reg asked.

Melissa shrugged. 'Things seemed to bring us together. It all seemed natural enough to me, at the time.'

' "At the time" – does it still seem so natural? Don't you think he might have had an ulterior motive by wanting to make you become an accomplice in his plans?'

Melissa shook her head and appeared to blink back tears. 'No!' she said emphatically. 'I think he just started to like me, and me him.'

'Were you lovers before you went with him on the punt, up the river?' Alison Knott asked softly. 'Or did it first happen that same night, the night Sir Gordon died?'

'We weren't lovers then and we're not lovers now. It may surprise you to know I've not had a lover yet. You can have a doctor check if you like. I don't care. I don't think Tiny's had a lover either, but that's only my feeling.'

137

'Are you telling us that an attractive girl like you was alone with him on that punt for the best part of three hours, and he didn't try and get fresh? Really?' Alison went on, her eyebrows raised as though such a thing was an utter impossibility.

Melissa stared at the far wall. 'I'm not saying anything like that. We're only human. Yes, we did kiss and cuddle. I didn't mind that, but we didn't have sex. Neither did he try to make me. I might have let him, if he had, but I don't know that. Tiny's got principles and good manners. I think he likes me too much to want to cheapen me.'

'Did you talk about Sir Gordon that night? You both must have hated him over that business with the cuneiform tablet. It must have been an awful shock to you when he took it so seriously and didn't laugh it off as you expected,' Reg suggested.

Tears formed in Melissa's big dark eyes. 'No! No! No!' she cried, each word coming out as a tiny explosion of frustrated anger. 'We didn't plant that thing. I don't know how it came to be there. Why don't you believe me? We didn't hate Sir Gordon, but he was wrong about us. Ever so wrong. I know trench "K" is being widened – haven't they found anything to prove that yet?'

'It'll be a couple of days before they get down to the right levels,' Reg explained. 'Never mind. So, that night on the river, you and Tiny must have tied up your punt at the end of Sir Gordon's garden, and then you both went up to the house, to reason with him,' Reg went on remorselessly. 'Why don't you tell us the truth? If Sir Gordon lost his temper and hit out at Tiny, you'd expect Tiny to defend himself, wouldn't you? That'd be perfectly understandable. It would have all been an accident then. With you as a witness the worst we could charge him with would be manslaughter. Tiny probably wouldn't even go to prison. Come on, admit it. That's what happened, isn't it?'

'No, it isn't,' Melissa shouted angrily and striking her knee with a fist in frustration. 'I never got out of that punt, not even for a minute, and neither did Tiny.'

'Oh come on,' Alison said sarcastically. 'Three hours in a boat, and Tiny had been drinking, even if it was only lemonade shandies. He must have had at least one call of nature, and if he's such a nice boy as you claim, he wouldn't have done that in front of you. He'd have gone on the bank, behind some bushes. Right?'

Melissa's eyes opened wide in confusion. 'I, er . . .' she muttered hesitantly.

'So, Tiny did go ashore. Where?' Reg demanded, his eyes narrowing. This was as near to a breakthrough as they'd come so far.

'It was dark, I can't be sure,' Melissa cried out, shaking her head.

'How long was he gone?' Reg went on.

'He wasn't gone above a minute, honestly,' Melissa whispered, looking thoroughly miserable.

'A minute, or two minutes – or three or five or ten? Were you wearing a watch? Could you see to tell the time? How do you know how long he was gone?'

'It wasn't long. Honestly, it wasn't long,' she cried out in despair.

She might have gone on to say more, but the interview was abruptly interrupted.

The door of the room was unceremoniously burst open, and framed in the doorway was a slim dark-haired girl whose dark eyes flared with anger.

'That's enough of that, you bloody coppers,' she said in an icily cold, Australian-accented voice. 'I can hear what's been going on in here through that wall. It's the third degree you're putting this poor kid under. You leave her alone. You lot aren't civilised. They don't even do that sort of thing in my country. Leave her alone and get out. If you want trouble, just try it on, mates. There's enough of us here to sort you two out. You'll be in the street with no pants on, if you don't watch it.'

'You tell them so, too,' cried the thin-faced grey-haired landlady, who'd come to join in the proceedings. 'I wouldn't have let them in if I'd've known who they was. I don't like coppers.'

Reg Finch stared at the dark girl's angry face. Others had joined her now, and they looked a distinctly hostile group. A rumpus with a load of girl students was the last thing he wanted. Anyway, they'd broken Melissa's story, and that was success enough for the moment. He put his papers in his case and stood up. Discretion was very often the better part of valour.

'We're just leaving. Thank you, Miss Fairbrother, you've been most helpful,' he said in as calm and confident a voice as he could muster. He politely manoeuvred Alison Knott to the doorway before him. That successfully shifted the Australian harridan out of the way, and enabled him to attain the safety of the bright outdoors while still wearing his trousers.

It had been a successful interview, but he didn't feel very pleased with himself at the way it had been achieved, all the same.

Jim Vine's shop was one of a row of four in the middle of a housing estate.

It was easy enough to spot, even from a distance. It had JIM THE BUTCHER in large black letters over the window.

'Mr Vine about?' Walsh asked the young man behind the counter, having waited patiently while the customer before him was being served.

The young man shook his head. 'He's having a few days off. Now, what would you like? I've got some nice cuts of real tasty beef. Been properly hung too, it has. Go on, treat yourselves. Your missus'll like that, won't you, love?' he went on, smiling at Brenda Phipps. 'Better'n the soggy cardboard you buys at the supermarket counter.'

'Thank you, no. It's Jim Vine we want. He lives in the flat above the shop, doesn't he? Is he in?' Walsh demanded.

The young man turned and shouted through the open door at the back of the shop. 'Mr Hutchinson! Feller here wants Jim.' Then he turned back to aim his cheerful sales patter at the next customer in the queue.

Mr Hutchinson was white-haired, rheumy-eyed, and well past retirement age. He blinked as he stared at Walsh's identity warrant card, then wiped his swollen reddened hands on his blue and white striped apron.

'Well, I don't rightly know where he's gone. He never said. He came round last night and asked me if I'd look after the shop for a few days. I does that for him, t'was me as had the shop before him, you see. He never said where he was going. He ain't done nothing wrong, has he? A nice lad, is young Jim. Everyone likes him.'

'Did he leave a telephone number, so you could contact him?' Brenda asked with a frown.

Hutchinson shook his head.

'He went off in his car, did he? Do you know the number and the make? Or did he use his motor bike?' Walsh wanted to know.

The young man had been listening intently while still serving the customers, and he answered those questions. 'His car and his two bikes are in the lock-up garage, out the back. Saw them there this morning. I've a key, you see. I puts me bike in there during the day. There's a lot of thieving beggars about, you know.'

'Have you a key to his flat? Maybe there's something there which might tell us where he's gone,' Walsh said, hopefully. It rather looked as though the bird, in the form of Jim Vine, had flown, and that in itself suggested guilt, or fear of something. When the sounds from the baying pack spread out over the countryside, plenty of creatures with no convenient safe bolt-hole panicked, broke cover and ran, with the inevitable reaction – anything that ran had to be chased. Unlike hounds though, the police as a pack were not in direct sight or smell of their quarry, and had the added problem of needing to pick out one particular fox from the millions who were roaming around, living their normal law-abiding lives.

They followed Hutchinson upstairs. The flat was reasonably tidy, and showed no obvious signs of a hurried departure; however, there was a noticeable lack of clothes in the drawers and airing cupboard, and no clean handkerchiefs or shirts at

141

all. The fridge in the kitchen was virtually empty, and there was no tinned food anywhere.

'He's definitely done a bunk, Chief,' Brenda observed regretfully, 'and it would appear he's made jolly sure he's left nothing behind to help us in any way. No photos, no papers, no address books, no passport.'

'You're sure you've no idea where he could have gone, Mr Hutchinson?' Walsh asked again.

Hutchinson shook his head. 'He's got a sister up Liverpool way, I've heard him talk about her, but he don't go to see her very often. No, it's normally every other Saturday I comes in for him, and then he's off with his tent and his motor bike, camping with his friends, but I'll tell you what else is missing. He had a pair of pistols hanging on that wall over there. Old flintlock pistols they were. Belonged to his dad, you know.'

'Pistols? Real ones, you mean? Did he have any powder and shot?' Walsh asked anxiously.

Hutchinson nodded his aged head vigorously. 'Oh aye, they were real enough, and he had some black powder in a little metal flask thing with a long cord you could hang round your neck. He could make his own shot too. He told me once how his poor old mum did her nut when he and his dad melted some old lead pipe over the gas stove, and made balls in a little mould he'd got.'

'Right, Brenda, we've got some work to do. We'll need a photo of him from somewhere and a full description, then we can get search teams organised to look for him. They can do the railway station, the bus companies, and so on, first. He's probably not on a borrowed motor bike, since his leather gear's still here. We'll get Forensic to check that over, particularly his boots.' Walsh was running through a check-list in his mind for the initial stages of organising a hunt for an armed man. Even if those flintlock pistols were old, they'd be lethal enough if you got in the way of one of their lead bullets.

'A photo's no problem, Chief,' Brenda interrupted with a rueful smile. 'Alison took plenty at the motor-bike rally. Vine's sure to be on one of them.'

'Good, you get on the phone to her and find out. While you're doing that I'll have a word with the neighbours, they might have seen him leave. Maybe there was a taxi, or someone gave him a lift. Then we'll have a chat with those two friends of his, the solicitor and the accountant. They must have tipped him off last night.'

'Oh aye,' said the wife of the greengrocer next door. 'He went out all right. I saw him from the window. He put two suitcases in his car, and drove off. About half-nine it was, or something like that. I always look through the window if we hear noises out the back. What with burglars and hooligans, one can't be too careful. He came back an hour or so later, though. I was getting ready for bed then. I didn't hear him go off after that, but he must have walked if his car's still there, mustn't he?'

'Certainly I spoke to him last night,' Graham Spencer the solicitor readily admitted, leaning confidently forward with his elbows on the desk in his spacious office. His eyes were cold as he stared back at his questioners, but his impassive face held no recognisable emotions.

'And why should I not?' he went on. 'He was as shocked as we were to learn that the girl we'd befriended at the rally was nothing but, if you'll pardon the expression, a snake in the grass. As for him taking a few days off when the fancy takes him, I can see nothing wrong in that. It's one of the advantages of being self-employed, to be able to come and go as one pleases. No, I'm unable to tell you where he is now, because I do not know.'

'Right, so there were no long-distance buses that Vine could have been on that late at night, but he could have caught a London-bound train, or one going north. See the man on duty at the ticket desk at the station – he may recognise the

143

photographs – and the man in "left-luggage". Vine must have taken his suitcases somewhere,' Walsh suggested. 'And to be on the safe side, check Heathrow and Gatwick for early flights this morning. He couldn't have obtained a ticket from a travel agent, so he'd have had to pay at the airport in cash or by credit card. That shouldn't present a problem, but what does is the possibility that he's gone to stay with someone locally.'

'He wouldn't need to take his own food with him if he was staying with someone else,' Arthur Bryant commented, his brow furrowed by the effort of concentration.

'Perhaps it's an empty place he knows of, some friend who's gone away for a few days,' Alison suggested.

'Either is a possibility, but it means you questioning his acquaintances and friends and following up any lead you get. Right?'

'Am I still doing the surveillance at Hinching Park tonight?' Arthur wanted to know.

Walsh shook his head. 'No, I'll find someone else for that. We're going to be busy enough trying to find this Vine fellow.'

'Don't forget, tonight is Beethoven night, boss,' Reg warned.

Walsh scowled. 'I hadn't, and we can't put that off. Gwen would murder me if we did. Alison and Arthur will have to do the best they can, on their own.'

# 14

Cambridge's Guildhall had its high interior walls and wide ceiling painted in various shades of cream and white. No doubt that was a decorator's ruse to give the whole a vaster sense of cavernous space than was perhaps due.

Nearly all the seats were occupied. At the far end, on a raised platform, were the orchestra, the choir, four soloists and, in command, the conductor.

At the start of the piece the very spaciousness of the hall had been a problem. The upper air was so still and lifeless that it was reluctant at first to assist the free passage of audio resonances, and as a result the orchestra had sounded thin and weak. Eventually, though, the sound-waves built up enough sympathetic vibrations for the building to become one huge sound-box, which then readily transmitted each subtle, sonorous sequence of notes.

Those sonorous subtle sequences of Beethoven's notes were being played well enough by the instruments of the orchestra to hold the attention of the audience in their timeless spell.

Now, in the final movement, the soloists were adding their vocal contribution, and the choir were on their feet too, at long last.

The conductor had grimaced at them a moment ago, while still waving his arms and baton vigorously. Those facial changes had warned them that their big moment was rapidly approaching. Chests heaved as deep breaths were taken into cramped lungs. Some even cleared their throats – noises that were cut off abruptly by violent digs in the ribs from alarmed neighbours.

The tenor was singing his piece with great enthusiasm. His head seemed to jerk backwards like some giant woodpecker on a tree as he exploded out each staccato syllable.

When he'd finished this bit, they would all come in.

The conductor looked up at them again, or perhaps it was to heaven for aid, or a miracle. Then he waved both arms wildly and clearly mouthed, 'Now!'

'FERN-en SERK-en DEE-fron VOLK-arh,' the chorus screamed and bellowed enthusiastically, immediately raising the decibel level way past the point at which a factory inspector would insist on ear protectors.

The German speakers in the audience shuddered noticeably.

Until now it had been pretty good, Walsh thought. The orchestra had given a remarkably mature and disciplined performance, considering how young they were. The soloists

145

were good too – probably they were professionals, giving their services free for a good cause.

The ladies and girls of the choir wore long royal blue satin gowns, with little puff sleeves, which looked rather silly. He'd spotted Lady Ingrid Lignum much earlier on. She was in the middle of the second row. Her high-cheeked Nordic features seemed to have aged somewhat since he'd last seen her, or perhaps that gaunt look was caused by the harsh lighting. She was still very attractive though, and it was difficult to imagine her as the brutal murderer of her husband. Of course, that was the humanist side of his nature speaking. It was nice to know that he still had some of that quality left, even after all his experiences of crime. He and his team had done their best to break down Lady Ingrid's alibi, or to find some male of her acquaintance who might have been an accomplice. All to no avail, as yet, but he wouldn't stop trying, not until the real murderer had been brought to book.

Over there, on the far side of the front row, was the Chief Constable, in dinner-jacket and bow tie, beside his school governor wife, permed, begowned and bejewelled as befitted her status.

Walsh felt tired, and he'd need to make the effort to give Gwen plenty of attention later; he hadn't seen much of her since he'd involved himself with the surveillance operation in North London. She was pretty understanding, but it wouldn't be wise to push her too far. Reg Finch, with his wife and the two young crippled girls from the orphanage, further down same row of seats, no doubt had much the same problem.

It was difficult, though, to stop one's brain pondering on a problem. If the butcher, Vine, was Lignum's murderer, and if the note to the Enfield fence had been initialled A.M. to put suspicion on MacGregor, how come Vine had known anything about MacGregor? There was no apparent link between those two, except that Vine's shop was only a mile or so from the excavation site in Hinching Park.

146

The final climax of the concert was now approaching. One could never quite be certain which sequence of Beethoven's crashing chords was going to be the last.

He was going to have to be sociable now and let Lignum's murder drop into the back of his mind for a while.


'I rather thought it might be a nice idea,' Walsh said when they were all standing together in the exit gangway, 'if we went and had something to eat, at McDonald's perhaps. Would you like that, Julie?' he asked, smiling down at the pretty blue-eyed eight-year-old. She looked up at Reg for assurance. He nodded and smiled.

'Thank you,' she said politely, yet obviously delighted at the prospect. 'That would be very nice.'

'Will you be able to walk that far, Julie?' Gwen asked solicitously, for Julie had an artificial left leg concealed by her trousers.

'Oh yes, no problem,' was the spirited reply.

Having set up the plan, there was little for Walsh to do, except follow behind and bring up the rear on his own. Reg and Margaret, with Julie between them, went on ahead and Gwen and Brenda both gave their attention to Julie's friend.

Outside it was a cooler evening than of late. The sky was overcast and there was just the hint of a fine drizzle in the air.

Fortunately McDonald's wasn't too far away, and not too crowded either. They pushed two tables together and sat round them in something like a party mood.

They'd hardly made themselves comfortable, though, when Brenda reached over and tugged at his sleeve.

'At the table in the corner, Chief. Behind you,' she whispered. 'Fairbrother and MacGregor.'

Walsh resisted the temptation to sigh audibly or to turn and stare. It seemed as if even this attempt at a private social life was to be marred by his job of seeking out criminals. He wasn't surprised that murder suspects and the police could come into such close proximity in off-duty hours, for

Cambridge wasn't a big city, and its centre was compact and active.

There was a mirror on the far wall and Walsh found that if he moved his chair a little he could see the pair reflected in that.

Their faces were turned towards his group, so obviously they recognised the police investigating team. They wouldn't be friendly looks. Reg had explained that he and Alison had been a bit hard on the girl that morning. That couldn't be helped; besides, there were plenty of grey areas with interview techniques as well as black and white ones, and whichever they'd used, they'd been successful in getting her to admit that MacGregor had left her for a short while on that fateful night. How significant that admission was, he'd yet to decide. That was another thing he hadn't had the time to think through properly.

'Well, did you enjoy the concert then, Sidney?' Gwen demanded, digging her husband ruthlessly in the ribs with her elbow.

Walsh blinked back to reality and found they were all looking at him.

'Sidney, you are becoming a dreamer in your old age. Julie asked if you enjoyed the concert,' Gwen went on remorselessly.

Walsh smiled sheepishly at Julie and gave her a slow conspiratorial wink, with the eye Gwen couldn't see.

'It was fine,' he said, 'until the choir joined in. Then it sounded as though a fox had got in among the chickens.'

At least it brought a few polite giggles. Julie had obviously thought he was being left out of the general conversation; that was why she'd asked the question. She really was a nice, thoughtful, well-mannered child.

He set himself to beam out a continuous, all-embracing, rather vacuous smile, while allowing his gaze to rest on whoever was speaking at the time. That ought to give the impression that he was attending to what was going on.

He stole another glance at that mirror. The girl, Melissa, appeared to be dabbing at her eyes with a handkerchief, while the boy was patting her arm consolingly.

He felt a wave of sympathy for the two youngsters who were so miserably caught up in the tangled web of a murder, but even so, the pressures and strains on them as suspects could not be eased until the real murderer was identified. He, the investigating officer, was not creating that pressure, it was endemic to the situation. That, as much as Reg's questioning, had brought about the change in the girl's story. Possibly MacGregor was now being told about that change. It would certainly increase his mental strain and worry. It was tough on him, but war was being waged, war against a ruthless killer, who needed to be brought to justice for the safety of society in general.

Jim Vine might have acknowledged his guilt by going into hiding, but when it came to motive and opportunity the circumstantial case against MacGregor was very strong too. One or two more little twists in Fairbrother's story might make that case conclusive. Reg would have to bring the girl to headquarters, to have her make a new official statement. There appeared to be aggressive anti-police elements in the house where she lived.

Brenda whispered loudly, 'They're going.'

Sure enough the two were on their feet, wriggling their arms into light windcheaters. Then they went out of his vision. He turned in his chair; there was no need to pretend not to be watching them now.

The pair stood outside the glass swing doors. MacGregor appeared to be wanting them to go together in one direction, but the girl was shaking her head; a hand held palm outward clearly indicated that she wanted to go the other way, alone. After a few moments she did just that. She walked slowly away with her shoulders bowed and as though each step was an effort. She presented a picture of despondency and depression.

MacGregor stood watching her for a few moments, then he too left, but in the other direction.

Walsh turned his attention back to his party. His beatific smile had gone now, and he found himself pinching his bottom lip between his thumb and his forefinger. He sensed both Brenda and Gwen looking at him momentarily, but neither spoke. He really wanted to be on his own, with time to think.

It might be a good idea, tomorrow, when Reg brought the girl, Fairbrother, in to take her new statement, for MacGregor to be brought in for questioning as well. Maybe they'd be able to play out that old game which was so often successful, and by convincing MacGregor that Fairbrother had cracked and was spilling the beans, draw out of him a complete confession.

Having made a firm positive plan of action, he suddenly felt much more relaxed.

The realisation that the conversation round the table was now about ordering more food and drinks brought a genuine smile to his face. It seemed that Julie and her friend intended to make the most of their treat, by trying as much of the varied menu as they could possibly stuff into their skinny little bodies.


This deep melancholy, and the desire to be miserable on her own, wasn't at all healthy, Melissa Fairbrother said to herself for the umpteenth time.

It was called depression, she realized that, but just giving it a name did nothing to alleviate its effects or its causes. She had made the effort to get out of her room for fresh air and exercise, and she'd unburdened her soul to Andrew. Talking about one's problems was supposed to be the right thing to do, but his obvious sympathy and understanding hadn't really helped, it had in fact served to emphasise the helplessness of the situation they were both in. That was the trouble, there was nothing she or Andrew could do about it. Everything was in the hands of someone else. She swung her foot to kick at a piece of litter. Even that was an effort. The desire to give up trying, and simply to sink into the darkness of oblivion, was becoming a strangely attractive proposition.

She walked straight across the road by St John's College without even looking for oncoming traffic, so engrossed was she in her morbid thoughts.

The driver of one car slowed noticeably, and wisely kept a very careful eye on this more than usually erratic Cambridge pedestrian.

Had she been more conscious of her surroundings Melissa would have turned down the lane by the old Round Church, that was the shortest way home, but by the time she had realised what she'd done, she had gone quite some distance on. It was no great matter, there were other passages suitable for those on foot.

The most attractive for a tourist would be the one by Magdalene Bridge, because of its views of the murky river and the manicured lawns of the college that named the bridge, on the opposite bank. There was a nearer passage though, more convenient if less picturesque, between a shop and a high building. She turned into that.

The faint sound of footsteps behind her failed to penetrate the incoherent mass of thought in her mind, but it did stimulate some primeval survival instinct in her brain. That alone caused her to tense up and turn her head. In the darkened gloom of the passage she saw what seemed to be a massive figure, with outstretched arms reaching for her. It was a quirk of the light perhaps, but the impression Melissa had in that split second of viewing was that the figure appeared to have no head.

Now she reacted positively – she screamed loud and shrill, and flung out a hand protectively. That hand made contact with something solid since pain shot up her forearm, but her turning so quickly had unbalanced her, and when the figure's hand grasped her arm and pulled, she fell towards the wall, hitting her head on the rough brick surface with such a stunning blow that her cries were cut off abruptly.

Perhaps that momentary period of unconsciousness was a good thing, for it meant that she felt no pain as the sharp thin-bladed knife in the ghastly figure's free hand was driven deep into her side.

It was fifteen minutes or so later when the pager on Detective Chief Inspector Walsh's compact mobile phone started its insistent bleeping. At that moment he was paying the bill at McDonald's cash desk.

'A coloured girl's been knifed, up near Magdalene Bridge,' he announced abruptly to Gwen and the others. 'I'm sorry, but we'll have to go.'

Gwen's face assumed a mask of impassive resignation, not dissimilar to the one Reg's wife, Margaret, had adopted. They'd both long since trained themselves not to show the irritation and annoyance they actually felt when such a thing happened, knowing that it might affect the morale of their respective husbands, and hence their ability to concentrate on their work and duty.

'Of course,' Gwen uttered perkily. 'Don't worry about us. We'll be all right.'

'You think it's Fairbrother, do you, Chief? Is she still alive?' Brenda asked, as the three of them walked hurriedly through the city centre and up Sidney Street.

'She was,' Walsh replied shortly.

He didn't want to waste his breath. Sitting about at the concert and then in McDonald's had stiffened his joints. Now, as he walked fast without actually running, the calf muscles in his legs were starting to twist into knots. He tried to relax and lengthen his stride, but that had no noticeable effect. Still, there wasn't far to go.

The white patrol car with the orange side stripes had its near wheels well on to the pavement; its rotating blue light flashed out a warning to the world at large and in particular to the dozen or so members of the public who had seemingly appeared from nowhere, like moths to a lighted candle.

There was little enough for them to see at the moment, though.

'The ambulance went off five minutes ago,' the patrol car driver said, holding his notebook up to the light so that he could read it better. 'The girl was knifed in the right side, just below the ribs. The paramedic didn't think it was fatal, but he got her on the drip pretty quick all the same. Not so much bleeding as you'd expect, but the girl was conscious in spite of the pain, and had kept her hand tight on the wound. She could talk sensibly enough, too. She said her name was Melissa Fairbrother, and she's a student, in rooms just round the corner, at number 9. Down there.' He pointed down the passage. 'She kept saying it wasn't Tiny. I didn't understand what she meant at first, but apparently that's the nickname of her boyfriend. How she could be so certain, I don't know, because she then went on to say that her attacker came up from behind, and that it was too dark to see clearly. She said she didn't see his face because the fellow didn't have one. Hardly surprising if she rambled a bit, she'd had a nasty bash on the side of her head as well. That's about it, sir.'

Walsh set about examining the full length of the passage in the light of the patrolman's torch, but found nothing that might give a clue as to the assailant's identity.

'Brenda,' he said eventually, 'you'd better get down to the hospital and find out what the latest situation is. Talk to her if you can. If they're already operating, get a message to the surgeons and ask them to give us their best description of the weapon used, will you?'

A wound on a dead person could be examined in detail by an expert, but in cases where an injury was not fatal, such interesting considerations took second place to the far more important task of saving lives.

'Come on, Reg,' he went on. 'We'll go and have a look round her room. That'll be a quicker way of finding her parents' address than by getting on to the college at this time of night. Then we'll go and have a few words with boyfriend Tiny, after we've set up a house-to-house inquiry round here – maybe someone saw or heard something.'


A small group of girls stood talking excitedly on the landing as Reg followed Walsh and the landlady up the stairs to Melissa's room.

The landlady's bunch of keys was not needed, since the door opened at a turn of the handle.

As Reg went in he noticed the slim dark-haired Australian girl pointing at him with a finger. What she was saying to the others he could not hear, but bearing in mind her previous outburst when he'd been there, it was probably not complimentary. He felt his face redden, and was glad to follow the others into the room, and close the door behind him.

'Letters or address book,' Walsh muttered, and pulled out the top drawer of the small chest.

The landlady stood in the middle of the room, arms folded across her chest, and glowered silently at her two visitors. Clearly such goings-on did not conform to her standards of gentility or propriety.

Reg Finch inspected the bookcase. His glance flitted quickly over the volumes in each row, his head turning from side to side like a chirpy sparrow's, since some titles read from the left-hand side, others from the right, but it was not his search that was successful.

'Here we are,' Walsh said, holding up a letter with the sender's name and address embossed at the top.

He proceeded to tap out the telephone number of Melissa's parents on his mobile phone.

'She's been taken to Addenbrooke's Hospital, in Cambridge. Yes, I understand she was alive and conscious when the ambulance left the scene of the incident. It was a knife wound. No, we haven't made an arrest. No, I can't tell you the full extent of her injuries, but I'm sure the hospital will, if you ring them directly,' he explained in answer to the questions of the shocked and bewildered Fairbrother parents.

'There's nothing else we can do here, boss,' Reg announced.

'No, a chat with young Tiny MacGregor is our next job,' Walsh said with a grim smile. 'I get the feeling things are starting to hot up a little bit, don't you?'


At that late hour the intricate wrought-iron gates of Downing College were drawn closed against the outside world. Access then was through the doors of the Porter's Lodge.

'Young MacGregor, Chief Inspector?' the black bowler-hatted porter repeated. He knew the two police officers, who were not infrequent visitors, but their expressions suggested that their presence here tonight was no social matter. He wondered what young Andrew MacGregor had been up to, to get on the wrong side of the law.

'He came in about a quarter of an hour ago, but you won't find him in his room, because he asked me to ring and find out if he could go and see Professor Hughes. That's where he probably is. Would you like me to find out?' he went on, reaching for his phone.

'Please,' Walsh said, looking at his watch impatiently. He would rather have seen MacGregor without the professor, or any other outsider, being there; it might have been easier to winkle the truth out of the boy then.

'The professor will be happy to see you, if you'd like to go up,' the porter said.

Professor Edwin Hughes's old-fashioned standards of politeness and courtesy were not impaired by anything so common as mere curiosity over the reasons for the presence of his two police visitors at that late hour. He ushered them into his rooms with his usual consideration, offered them refreshment and saw them seated comfortably before sitting down himself. Then he beamed a disarming smile at Walsh.

'I gather you wish to talk to young Andrew here,' he said. 'I am quite happy to absent myself, if you so wish. However, if I am permitted to remain, I will, of course, not interrupt or interfere.'

Walsh inclined his head slightly in acknowledgement, and turned to study the occupant of a nearby chair. Andrew MacGregor's face looked tired and drawn. Obviously, as with the Fairbrother girl, the mental strains of the past few days had undermined his youthful resilience.

'Andrew,' Walsh said eventually, 'I'd like you to tell me where you went after leaving McDonald's this evening.'

Both MacGregor and Hughes looked surprised at this apparently innocuous question.

'I, er, went down to the river, by King's. I sat on the bank for a while, to do a bit of thinking,' MacGregor replied hesitantly.

'You needed to do some thinking, didn't you, because you'd just learned that Melissa Fairbrother had knocked a great hole in your story about events on the night Sir Gordon died,' Walsh suggested. 'Why did you tell us you hadn't got out of the punt, when you had?'

'I'm sorry. I genuinely forgot about it. I didn't think it was significant. I wasn't gone above a minute, honestly.'

'Where did you go after King's, tonight? Did you meet anyone?'

MacGregor looked down at his fingers. 'I didn't go anywhere else. When I left there, I came straight here. I can't remember seeing anyone I know, but then I wasn't looking particularly.'

'So you didn't go anywhere near Magdalene Street?'

'Good Lord, no.'

'I'll ask you again, because you seem forgetful at times. After you left Melissa Fairbrother outside McDonald's this evening, did you then go anywhere near Magdalene Street?' Walsh demanded.

'No, I didn't,' MacGregor replied firmly, frowning deeply at his tormentor. 'But why all these questions about Magdalene Street?' The frown deepened into alarm. 'Melissa lives near there. Has anything happened to her?' he went on anxiously, his fingers starting to twitch nervously.

'You could say that.' Reg Finch spoke for the first time. His face was stern and implacable as he watched the boy's face, trying to distinguish innocent reactions from those of an actor. 'On her way home she was attacked by a big man with a knife, and left for dead.'

'Good God!' MacGregor exclaimed, appearing to be overcome with dismay, just as a good actor should.

'It hasn't escaped our notice that you're a big man, but in my young days we didn't leave our girlfriends to walk home on their own in the dark,' Finch said coldly. 'We took them to their front door, and saw them safely in.'

'But she insisted,' MacGregor blurted out, his face reddening with emotion. 'She said she wanted to be alone. I tried to persuade her, but I couldn't force her, could I?'

'No, you couldn't force her,' Reg went on, 'but you could have followed well behind her, keeping her in sight until she did get home. Is that what you did? Follow Melissa home, I mean?'

'No, I didn't. I wish now that I had. Poor Melissa. Who'd want to kill her? Why?' MacGregor put his face in his hands, and his broad shoulders gave a heave. An audience might well have applauded if such a scene were enacted on a stage.

Professor Hughes leaned back in his chair. His natural curiosity had been the real reason for his wanting to be in on this interview, but the way it had developed had been quite unexpected. He would have liked to ask questions, but he stuck to his promise, and said nothing.

There was silence for a few moments, then Walsh spoke.

'Andrew MacGregor, I'm not arresting you, but I would like you to fetch a change of clothes from your room, and then come with us to the police station. I believe you can help us with our inquiries. The professor can come with you, if you and he wish, or you may have a solicitor.'

MacGregor lifted his head. His face was red and blotchy now, and his eyes were wet with tears. He stood up, but he didn't protest, or say anything.

'I will come with him,' the professor said quietly, 'but if Sergeant Finch could go with Andrew to collect the change of clothes from his room, might I have a few words with you alone, Chief Inspector? We can meet them downstairs in the quadrangle.'

'A good idea,' Walsh nodded.

'Sergeant Finch only said that Melissa was left for dead. Is she dead? Or was that the impression you wanted Andrew to form?' Professor Hughes asked.

Walsh smiled grimly. 'She's being operated on in the hospital, but the doctors seem fairly confident that she'll live.'

'Well, that's one good thing then,' Hughes said with obvious relief. 'Was she conscious when she was found? Did she see her assailant?'

'Yes, she was conscious, but we haven't had the opportunity to question her properly yet,' Walsh replied.

Hughes nodded. 'And Andrew's change of clothes?'

'I want Forensic to do tests on the ones he's wearing, and on his hands, face and fingernails,' Walsh explained. 'If there are traces of Melissa's blood on him, or anything else to link him with this attack, we'll keep him for further questioning. If not, we'll probably let him go – for the time being. Naturally we'll try and corroborate his story, but he hasn't given us much to go on, has he?'

The professor looked glum, and changed the subject. 'Things look somewhat grim, I'm afraid. I had hoped that when Charles Choosely and his team finally got to the critical layers in the excavation of that trench, they would find something to substantiate MacGregor's and Fairbrother's story of the cuneiform tablet, but that won't happen until the day after tomorrow, I gather.'

'How did you learn that, professor?' Walsh asked with a slight smile.

'Andrew told me, just before you arrived. His friends keep him informed on events at the excavations.' His eyes narrowed and he stared at Walsh shrewdly. 'If there are no traces of blood on Andrew's hands or clothing, Inspector, I do think that events on that site, over the next few days, might yet have some bearing on the murder of Sir Gordon.'

The professor was a very shrewd man, quite capable of putting various combinations of two and two together and getting any number of answers, one of which might be right. However, with this case of the murder of Sir Gordon Lignum, the professor lacked some of the vital information on which to base his projections.

He knew nothing of Jim Vine and the Mad Dogs, for instance. From Walsh's point of view both MacGregor and Vine were red-hot joint favourites, in a race in which the other runners noticeably lacked substance and form.

However, Walsh did not feel like extending the conversation further, so he merely smiled and said, 'You might well be right.'

# 15

'They murdered his Ninth, didn't they? Poor old Ludwig must still be turning in his grave. If they'd done his Fifth or Sixth, they wouldn't have had a choir to come in and ruin it for them,' the Chief Constable pronounced authoritatively. 'The kids in the orchestra weren't bad at all. I was most surprised. Never mind! So Forensic found no traces of the girl's blood on MacGregor's hands or clothing? That's a pity,' he went on as he sipped his early morning coffee. 'Still, he could easily have had his hand in a plastic bag as he held the knife, that would have been protection enough. Then he could have slipped across the road into St John's, over the Bridge of Sighs, and along by the river towards King's. That's where the knife is, more than likely – at the bottom of the river.'

'Maybe, but St John's main gate was closed by that time. He'd have had to go in through the lodge, and the porter doesn't remember seeing him,' Walsh explained.

'He's got an old car, hasn't he? Maybe he'd got that parked somewhere nearby.'

'That would suggest he'd planned the attack beforehand, yet he didn't know his girlfriend was changing her story until they were sitting in McDonald's. That's when Fairbrother says she told him.'

The C.C. shook his big balding head. 'Just because she's been knifed you're assuming she's innocent. Before then you reckoned she was his accomplice, because she must have known he'd planted the cuneiform tablet. If she was lying about one thing she's probably lying about the lot. Myself, I think it dawned on MacGregor that Fairbrother was going to spill the beans some time or other, so he planned to bump her off anyway. He's a Scot, isn't he? He probably carries his skean-dhu, or whatever they call a sheath knife up there, tucked in his sock. He knifed her with that, most likely.'

'Well, if you're right, he botched it. He won't get another opportunity, not while she's in Addenbrooke's,' Walsh added confidently.

'No, you must keep someone watching her night and day. Don't take any risks there, for heaven's sake,' the C.C. said emphatically. 'Now, you say you've let MacGregor run free because you think he might try and dig up this widened trench at the archaeological site tonight? I can't see why he'd bother. If the tablet was planted, there'd be nothing for the excavators to find, but if it was genuine, they might find something to prove it. Then no one could say he'd killed Lignum in order to keep him quiet.'

'True, but that's just the point. At the moment his best defence is to take the line that destroying the site would be the last thing he'd want to do. It wouldn't be difficult to make a jury believe that it was done by a third party, someone unknown. The site developers, for instance, or even one of these motor cyclists creating a red-herring to divert attention from their man Vine,' Walsh explained. 'Anyway, someone dug the site over before, and tonight's the last chance they'll get to do the same thing again, so we'll be watching in force.'

The C.C. nodded, somewhat reluctantly, and changed the subject. 'This motor cyclist, Vine, is armed with a couple of old saddle pistols, is he? Well, one of those things can be just as lethal as a rifle, if it hits you in the right place. If you find him, take all the proper precautions. Get the sharpshooters and flak jackets out, and keep everyone well away. Don't let anyone do anything stupid. I don't want anyone hurt. Right?'

'This report from the Met about the developers of the Huntingdon site is completely negative. They were hoping to get a tip-off from one of their underworld informers, but that hasn't happened,' Walsh explained regretfully. 'So there's no progress in that area. Now, we've reviewed the case against MacGregor as it stands, and we're happy we're doing the right things, so let's consider the matter from another point of view. Is there anyone else working on that site who might have had a grudge against either Lignum, MacGregor or Fairbrother? Reg, you've got the file of the interview reports of the other students – is there anything in them that strikes you as unusual or interesting?'

Reg was feeling tired, but he set about marshalling his thoughts into some kind of order; while he was doing that the fingers of his right hand drummed out a soft staccato on the top of Walsh's desk.

'I wish you wouldn't make that irritating noise, Reg. It's a bad habit you've got into,' Brenda said testily.

Walsh and Reg exchanged silent meaningful glances. Walsh's conveyed the message that her remark was best ignored, but Reg's expressed quite clearly his intention that any verbal attack on him would be returned, with interest.

He reached the offending hand to tug at the hair on the top of his head.

'Your eyes need testing, girl,' he said coldly. 'Bad habits are worn by dirty monks, and I've no tonsure, and I'm not celibate either.'

Just calling Brenda 'girl' would niggle her. She hated that.

'Very funny, old boy,' Brenda snapped back. 'A tonsure won't be long coming, you're getting mighty thin on top.'

'Cut out the wisecracks,' Walsh butted in sternly. 'Reg, do you reckon any of those other students might have had a grudge against Lignum, Fairbrother or MacGregor?'

Reg picked up the file, but he didn't open it.

'There's nothing specific, but there is one character. He wasn't on the site when the tablet was found, but he was there the day before. I met him when I went to talk to Professor

Gladsbury. He's a bit of a loner, with a rather cutting sense of humour, a bit like Brenda's. He makes his jokes with a straight face and no smile. He might be just the type to –'

'Lord,' Brenda interrupted, 'if we've got to write down the names of all the people with a more advanced sense of humour than yours, we'll have a list a mile long.'

'Pack it in, Brenda,' Walsh snapped irritably. 'You go and see your loner, Reg –'

He was interrupted by the ringing of the telephone.

The search for Jim Vine had included checking the movements of boats on the River Great Ouse, and its tributaries. The duty officer now told him that earlier that morning a small river cruiser had come up to Clayhithe, on the River Cam near Waterbeach, and that the lone man on board fitted the description of Jim Vine.

The man had gone shopping at the local store, then he'd topped up his water tank and petrol tank, cast off, and headed back downstream.

The report had been made by a retired Water Board worker, who lived near the old lock-keeper's cottage. He'd been visited the evening before by a police patrol, and been shown a photo of the missing man.

'We'll need a boat. See what you can find, and tell the two marksmen to get themselves ready,' Walsh asked of the duty officer, then he opened out a large-scale map on his desk.

It was relatively simple to plan the capture of a fugitive in a car. Any number of police vehicles could quickly be summoned by radio, and directed to watch all possible routes. However, planning the apprehension of a boat on the River Cam below Waterbeach suddenly became more complicated than it at first appeared.

The map showed that until Ely, ten or twelve miles further on, access to the river by road or land was not easy. The speed of boats was perhaps four or five miles an hour, so if Vine kept on downstream, Ely was two hours or more away, but he might never get there. He could turn back up the Ouse where it converged with the Cam, or there were umpteen smaller streams or dykes he could go up instead.

Walsh's fingers drummed on his desk while he thought out alternative lines of action. His involuntary action brought no comment from Brenda.

The force he needed was ready to hand. Two rifle marksmen, and he, Brenda and Reg would have hand guns. That would be enough, at this stage. Logically he needed one boat coming fast upriver from Ely and another going down from Waterbeach. Vine would be caught in the middle, but that would mean dividing his force, which would be unwise and take more time.

The duty officer had located a cabin cruiser at Clayhithe that was available immediately, if Walsh wanted it.

He did.

He arranged for police officers from Ely to send a boat upriver, with orders to merely watch and wait from a distance, if they caught up with Vine first, and also gave instructions for a watcher to be placed on each of the few river bridges.

He remembered the saying that a stern chase was a long chase, but discarded it as irrelevant. Vine wasn't running away now. As far as he was concerned, he was already in hiding. He'd have to get stores occasionally, certainly, but otherwise he'd find some little out-of-the-way backwater, and keep as much out of sight as he could.

They spent some minutes sorting out binoculars, loudhailers and first-aid kits, hand guns and flak jackets, then got on their way.


It was a fairly old cabin cruiser, painted white, except for the woodwork round the cabin top and inside the rear cockpit, which was varnished. From the bank it looked too high-sided to be stable, but it had a broad beam, and felt safe enough when one got on board.

Reg Finch took the little wheel and sent the vessel phutting downstream. His extra few inches of height gave him a good view forward over the cabin top. He eased the throttle further forward, and the angled bow-wave started surging and thudding into the muddy banks.

163

Walsh watched a gnarled and twisted willow as they went past. They were going much faster than a good walking pace. Five miles or possibly six miles an hour. A pair of moorhens with five young chicks tried to get out of the way of the wash. They rose and fell three feet and looked distinctly discomfited by the experience.

'Ease the speed back a bit, Reg. The odd mile an hour's not going to make much difference,' Walsh grunted, but Reg was already doing that. He'd seen a narrow, steep-sided drainage ditch joining the river on the right. They stared up it as they went past.

There was nothing down there, except a crude structure of wooden beams topped with strands of rusty barbed wire, placed, presumably, to prevent those of the boating community with a wanderlust from exploring the local farmer's fields. It was understandable, for this stretch of the river, with its high monotonously deserted banks, was decidedly lacking in any of those features which might delight the avid sightseer.

Still, it was a nice day to be out in a boat. There were plenty of blue patches between the puffy white clouds, and the sun, when it was out, made the little cockpit quite warm, but even so, there was a surprisingly cool breeze rippling the surface of the water.

It was a funny old job this, being a Criminal Investigation Officer. There were periods of routine when he was bound to his office by paperwork, but predicting what other things he might get up to in a day was about as difficult as guessing which way the coloured glass slivers might fall in a turning kaleidoscope.

Last night it had been a sociable concert, followed by the Fairbrother knifing. This morning he'd seen the C.C., had a brief case review session, and now he was on a peaceful river trip in the sunshine, with a loaded Smith & Wesson in his pocket, hunting a possible murderer.

He ought to find such changes amusing, but he didn't. He couldn't relax and enjoy them. The need to be alert and to concentrate all the time prevented that.

Reg was doing all the real work at the moment, by watching out for drainage channels and other places where a boat might be hidden.

Brenda and one of the marksmen had also stayed in the cockpit.

The marksman, a man with lean solemn features and dark eyes, was in his early thirties and had recently transferred from Wolverhampton. He sat frowning sternly at the water going past, and biting his fingernails.

'Are you all right?' Walsh asked gruffly.

The man looked startled for a moment.

'Sure,' he replied.

'Done this sort of thing before?'

It was an unnecessary question. To get on the marksman list, and to stay there, required continuous careful training.

He shrugged his shoulders and gave an exaggerated yawn. 'I've never had to fire a shot for real, yet.'

'Hopefully, it won't be necessary this time, either,' Walsh replied conversationally, and turned his attention to Brenda.

She too sat frowning, but there was a concerned look on her face which made Walsh scowl with annoyance. He had more than enough problems and responsibilities on his shoulders, without having to worry about the mental state of his supporting team.

'What the hell's the matter with you?' he said sternly.

She looked at him steadily with her large brown eyes and stopped pinching her lower lip between her fingers.

'I'm not happy with all this,' she said abruptly, waving a hand vaguely towards the marksmen. 'Sharpshooters and Smith & Wessons. It's not the right way.'

'Don't be damned silly,' Walsh replied scornfully. 'It's standard practice. The fellow's armed, isn't he? Even if it is with a couple of old pistols. Why did he take them if he wasn't prepared to use them?'

'That's precisely what worries me – he might be prepared to use them.'

'Well, what are you getting all broody about, then? He'll be clearly warned. Not once, but several times, and be told that

165

if he points a pistol at any one of us, then he's liable to be shot by our marksmen. He'll have the chance to disarm himself. You know the ropes. I don't see what's bothering you.'

He turned irritably away to pick up the binoculars and lean his elbows on the cabin top, while he set about scanning the banks further up the river.

'I don't think he's got those pistols to defend himself against us, Chief. I think he may have brought them to use on himself, if he gets in a tight corner. I think he might be suicidal.' Brenda spoke the words with an unaccustomed hesitancy.

Walsh continued staring through the binoculars. He now felt hot and bothered, and he had to force his mind to reason sensibly. Of course there was always the possibility that a cornered armed suspect might, at the last resort, use his weapons on himself. That was an aspect taken into account by police officers in siege training. The priorities were clear and simple enough, though. He allowed his mind to go through them. Firstly, to ensure the safe release of hostages, if any, then to achieve disarmament and surrender by verbal communication, using the right conciliatory words and in such a way as to calm aggression and emphasise the pointlessness of continued resistance. At all times, though, the safety of the public and of the police officers involved was paramount. That meant shooting Vine, if he ignored the warnings and appeared to be going to shoot an officer. One could hardly threaten to shoot him if it appeared that he was going to shoot himself. It would be rather pointless; either way would probably be fatal. What Brenda was really suggesting was that it might be more appropriate to use those psychological techniques needed when confronting someone who was already perched precariously on the edge of a high cliff, so to speak, and threatening to jump.

Now he had a big problem. How was he to combine the positive approach towards an armed murder suspect with the sympathetic understanding needed to thwart a potential suicide?

The words Brenda had spoken amounted to an official warning of specific complications. He could not ignore them.

If he were to do so, and Vine were to kill himself, even if the subsequent inquiry absolved him of blame, in his own mind he would feel guilty for the rest of his life.

He put the binoculars down and turned round.

'Are you sweet on this fellow, or something?' he asked aggressively, but that was merely to give himself more time to think.

'No,' she said, shaking her head. 'I'm just concerned about a fellow human being, who may be perfectly normal most of the time, but unstable on occasions when under severe mental and emotional stress. I think his two friends know that, and have tried to protect him.'

'He might also be a murderer. His so-called friends must think that, if they encouraged him to do a bolt.'

'They might, but it's also possible they just wanted to keep him out of our way, until Lignum's murder was solved,' Brenda persisted, and found an ally in Reg, who'd obviously been listening.

'She's quite right, boss,' Reg said, 'and I ought to remind you that you haven't organised a stand-by ambulance yet.'

'I know I haven't,' Walsh snapped. 'But it's pointless having an ambulance waiting at Clayhithe, if we don't come up against him until we're nearly in Ely, isn't it? Right, what do either of you suggest we do? I'm not going to take the risk of any of us getting hurt.'

'I've been thinking about that, Chief,' Brenda acknowledged. 'I think we ought to set up the marksmen as normal, and then let me approach him openly, and get as close as I can so that I can talk to him easily. He knows me, and I don't think he'd harm a woman, or even commit suicide in front of one either. What I do think would be wrong would be to isolate him by bellowing at him through the megaphone, telling him he's surrounded and he'll be shot if he doesn't do this, that and the other.'

'That sounds sensible enough to me, boss,' Reg agreed.

'I'll think about it. We haven't found him yet,' Walsh said non-committally, and proceeded to fill his pipe.

167

It was twenty minutes later when they spotted him, a long way down a straightish reach of the river. He was sitting on the right-hand bank, by a small willow tree, fishing.

'That's him,' Brenda confirmed as she stared hard through the binoculars.

Reg slowed the cruiser right down, and headed for the bank on the opposite side to Vine.

Vine's boat had been drawn into a small stream or channel; its stern just showed through the willow's hanging tresses.

'Right! So this is what we'll do,' Walsh stated in a positive voice. 'You two marksmen walk along the field behind the bank on this side of the river. One of you get to the far side of him. Find good positions where you can see him clearly, and settle yourselves down. We'll then go over to the other side, and Brenda and I will approach as near as we can to him, without taking risks. Then we'll start talking to him. How we go about things after that will depend on how he reacts. We'll leave our radios on, so you can hear all that's being said.'

'Brenda's got to go because he knows her, but two of you will widen the target,' Reg warned.

'I don't care. I've got to be where I can see what's going on,' Walsh said flatly. 'Reg, you can get on to headquarters. Tell them we've found Vine, and get them to send an ambulance and a doctor to Clayhithe, just in case.'

Brenda looked a strangely lopsided Wild West figure, as she walked along the bank. She was wearing the grey flak jacket like a long body-warmer, but because it had no pockets her Smith & Wesson was tucked into the one in the side of her jeans, and the jacket was rucked up, to make the butt free to be grasped quickly, if necessary.

Jim Vine still sat on his folding stool, fishing, although he'd turned his head several times to watch the strange manoeuvrings of the approaching boat and its occupants.

'That's quite near enough,' Walsh muttered, when they were about fifty feet away.

'A bit nearer, Chief,' Brenda insisted, carrying on walking. 'I can't talk to him this far away.'

At forty feet Walsh gripped her arm. 'No closer,' he insisted.

Brenda shrugged her shoulders and stood still.

'Hello, Jim! Are you all right?' she called out.

Jim Vine turned his head to look at her. 'Sure. How are you?'

'I'm fine. We want to talk to you, Jim, but we're not coming any closer because we think you've got a couple of pistols. Is that right?'

'Yes. Who's the bloke with you, Brenda?'

'He's my boss, Chief Inspector Walsh. He's a good man, Jim. You can trust him. Are the pistols loaded?'

'Yes. What's that sticking out of your pocket?'

'It's a 38-calibre Smith & Wesson, Jim. Where are your pistols?' Brenda called.

'In my fishing bag,' he replied, and he appeared to nod down at the grey canvas holdall in the grass at his feet. 'Those two on the other bank, they've got rifles with telescopic sights – are they aimed at me?'

'They are, Jim. I'm sorry, but we've got to do it. It's standard procedure when approaching an armed person, you see. Everything will be all right if you don't make any sudden moves, and don't reach for that bag. We don't want any trouble. Do you?'

Jim Vine shook his head slowly, but his body seemed to sag a little in the middle. His voice drifted softly on the wind, as though he were merely talking to himself. 'I can't believe all this,' he appeared to be saying. 'What is happening to me? First they think I've murdered someone I don't even know, and now if I move, they'll shoot me. What the hell's going on, Betty?'

'Betty was his wife's name, Chief,' Brenda whispered.

Walsh certainly looked worried now.

'Go easy with him, Brenda. You were quite right. If he's still talking to a wife who's been dead for years, his mind must be in a right mixed-up state. You'd better talk commonplace things. Ask him about his fishing or his motor bikes, anything like that might divert and settle his mind. There's no need to hurry, we've got plenty of time.'

169

These situations were always highly unpredictable. They could go on for minutes, hours or even days. Patience was needed – and constant vigilance. 'Keep awake, everyone,' Walsh warned into the radio.

'You like fishing, do you, Jim?' Brenda called out. At first there was no response, so she repeated the question even louder.

'The doctor said that when I got uptight, I ought to go fishing or do something quiet and peaceful,' he replied.

'He's had some counselling, then,' Walsh muttered.

'Caught anything?' Brenda yelled.

'Oh yes,' he replied, and he leaned forward on his stool to reach for his catch-net – or was it for one of the pistols in the fishing bag?

Everything happened far too quickly then.

'Don't do it, Jim,' Brenda screamed out, starting to run towards him, only to find herself suddenly falling forward on to her hands. Walsh had given her a mighty shove in the back, before he himself dropped flat on the grass. At the same time, there came the flat dull crack of a rifle shot.

Through the blades of grass at ground level Brenda saw Jim Vine's body seem to jerk in his bent-forward position, then his arms start to wave about wildly as he tried to regain his balance, but he did not succeed, and he gradually toppled over, and fell head first into the river.

# 16

'The water was only about three or four feet deep, close up against the bank,' Walsh explained, 'but the poor sod went in head first and got all tangled up in his catch-net – and he cracked his head on something in the mud, which knocked him out cold for a while. We thought the bullet had hit him, so we jumped in to hold his head above water until Reg brought the boat down, but there wasn't a scratch on him, except where he'd hit his head.'

170

'So, one of our highly trained, experienced marksmen missed from a range of less than a hundred yards, did he? A fat lot of use he was.' The Chief Constable frowned deeply. 'I'm damned if I know whether to be thankful he didn't kill the beggar or angry that he's such a lousy shot.'

Walsh ran his hand through hair still wet from a necessary shower, and sniffed. He'd had to sit around in his wet clothes for the best part of an hour, while the river cruiser had struggled its way back upstream to Clayhithe. As Sod's Law dictated, during that period the sun had gone behind the clouds and the cool breeze seemed to drop five degrees in temperature. From such circumstances colds developed, even in someone as fit and healthy as he thought himself to be.

'In a way it was a good thing. That shot certainly brought the whole situation to an abrupt end,' Walsh said with half a smile. 'Otherwise we might still have been sitting there.'

'I suppose so,' the C.C. agreed reluctantly, 'but since you haven't questioned this Vine fellow yet, you still don't know if it was all worth the effort.'

'True, but there'll be plenty of time for that tomorrow. The doctor said it was only mild concussion, and he's safe enough in Addenbrooke's.'

'This shooting, though,' the C.C. said seriously. 'We'll have to hold an inquiry. Was our man justified in firing, do you think?'

Walsh nodded. 'Vine certainly made a sudden movement towards the bag where he said his pistols were. I think he was only after his catch-net, myself, but I could only see a side view. From near enough front on it might have appeared different.'

'Well, you get reports from each one who was there, and let me have them. What are your plans now?'

'I'm setting up a comprehensive surveillance of that archaeological site for tonight. If the pattern of events on this case continues, then I hope someone will be out to destroy the bottom layer of trench "K" by digging it over, but whether it'll be Lignum's killer or not, I don't know,' Walsh admitted.

'Well, the best of luck. I don't fancy your chances, myself, but at least you know two of the people it won't be –

171

Fairbrother and Vine. Not with our people watching over them in Addenbrooke's Hospital, it won't.'


'This site is far too big for us to cover all possible ways of approach,' Walsh said at the final briefing. 'However, if whoever is going to come, comes by car and doesn't want to walk too far, then obviously they might park on the main road here.' He pointed to a spot on the large-scale map. 'There's a ditch and a hedge to negotiate, but it's not too difficult. Or they may come in from the other side, along this track and down by this field. That's the main access route for vehicles. However, there's a gate to the field that's always closed by the last person off the site. There's no lock or chain, but they'd have to stop and open it. So we'll have watchers at both of those places to give us advance warning. However, you could get at the site from a dozen other spots. These woods to the north are supposed to be private property, but kids play in there, and people from the estate walk their dogs –'

'That's the estate where Jim Vine's shop is, isn't it?' Brenda asked.

'That's right, but more importantly, just next to it is the posher area, where his two old school chums have their executive-type four-bedroomed houses.' Walsh smiled, giving Alison Knott the impression that in the Chief Inspector's mind, those two were the most likely to turn up later that evening.

She shrugged her shoulders. It would be a fair bet, she thought, since they were the last ones known to have seen Lignum alive.

'So the most sensible thing for us to do is to concentrate our attentions on the excavation site itself. Arthur Bryant is watching there now. His favourite place is about here, on the north side, nearest to Jim Vine's estate. When we get there, I'll take that place over, and he can take up station nearer to the main road. Alison, you can take your place to my left, somewhere here. Brenda and Reg have the south side to cover. There's a badger set in there somewhere, apparently, so

172

if you're very quiet you might see them, but I doubt it, they'll probably scent us and won't venture far. Now, the weather forecast is that it will remain dry and that the cloud will start to break up around midnight. Then there might be patchy moonlight, so we should have no problem spotting them when they move into the open. Once they make their intentions clear, by removing the trench covers and getting ready to dig, we move in and apprehend them. If they break and run, we must catch them before they get back into the trees, otherwise we could be floundering around in there for the rest of the night, and still lose them. So be positive, tackle hard round the legs so that they fall, then hang on tight until someone else gets there to help. Brenda and Alison will have the flash cameras; one or other should get a clear picture. The rest of us must keep our eyes on the intruders, otherwise when the cameras flash we'll lose our night vision. For the same reason, use your torches only when necessary. Now, you'll need time to get yourselves in position. Brenda and Reg will be dropped off here, to the south. Alison and I, here, to the north. I want us all in our places by nine thirty. Radio checks then every half-hour. Dark clothes are the order of the day, and hands and faces must be blackened too. It'll be chilly come the early hours, so wear something warm, but don't make yourselves so comfortable that you start dozing off. It could be a long night.'

'I've been after a long knight for years, but one in shining armour,' Alison whispered to Brenda. 'It sounds as though we're going into battle.'

'So we are, but you remember all that's been said,' Brenda warned softly. 'Details are important and when it comes to organising ambushes, the Chief is about the best in the business.'


'Good Lord, you startled me,' Arthur Bryant whispered as Walsh suddenly loomed out of the darkness, near where he sat beneath the tall Scots pine.

173

'Everything all right?' Walsh asked gruffly. His throat felt a little sore. He'd had a Beecham's before coming out, hoping that might stave off the development of a cold. He also wore a second sweater as well as a thick woolly fisherman's hat pulled well down over his forehead.

'I thought I saw something move in the bushes over there a little while ago, sir,' Arthur replied, pointing roughly towards the place where Reg Finch ought to be settling himself down, 'but I've seen nothing since.'

'Right. Now you move on towards the road,' Walsh instructed. 'If our man comes in that way, it'll be your job to cut off his retreat, but not until I give the word, mind.'

Bryant wriggled off on elbows and knees – how, he imagined, a Red Indian of old might have crawled. Such a method of progression became very tiring after only a short distance, but since he'd only adopted it to impress the Chief Inspector, he forced himself to continue in that manner until he arrived at his new position.

Walsh poured himself half a cup of hot coffee and settled down with his back against the tree. His eyes were becoming adjusted to the darkness now, and he found that if he concentrated hard he could make out many of the details on the open area before him: the light-coloured tarpaulins spread over the excavation areas, the dark mass of the small wooden hut in which were stored the excavators' tools and wheel barrows, and on the far side of the clearing, the shrubs and trees of the wood, which now concealed both Brenda and Reg. Young Arthur's eyes must be much better than his own, if he could see actual branches moving with the naked eye, but probably he'd used his night glasses. Walsh used his own to scan along the tree-line. It was like peering through a periscope into the eerie green depths of an underwater world.

He was going to have to make a decision about young Arthur Bryant very soon. His probationary period with the CID was coming to an end. Soon he should either be made a permanent member of the department, or rejected back into another branch of the force. The boy was an enigma in some

174

ways. Of his keenness there was no doubt. He would tackle all the tasks given him with enthusiasm, and, to be fair, he usually carried them out quite satisfactorily. The main criticism of him was his inability, sometimes, to report and communicate with any verbal fluency. It was as though he had difficulty preparing what he was going to say into a logical sequence. As a result he often didn't start at the beginning, and then, having to backtrack, he'd get himself confused. Yet his written reports were excellent. He was a bright enough lad, with a reasonable sense of humour too.

Walsh brought his mind back to the task in hand. The field of vision through the glasses was too narrow for general surveillance, and they quickly made his eyes ache. It was better if he used them intermittently.

He leaned back and took in deep breaths of the cool fresh night air. It really was pleasant to sit in such isolation, with nothing else to do other than watch and think, and savour the faint smells of pine and damp earth and listen to the musical sounds of the light breeze rustling through the leaves. Those musical sounds could only be heard by his left ear, since his right one contained a tiny speaker, which, with the lead from the throat microphone, was connected to his radio and formed his ethereal contact with the other world that at the moment seemed less real than this one.

It was at about eleven o'clock that the right-ear speaker made soft communicating noises.

'Reg here,' they said. 'We've got a visitor, boss. I've heard him, but I can't see him yet. He's somewhere to my right. That's your left, Brenda.'

'Thank you, Reg. I had worked that out,' came Brenda's voice. 'I can see him now. He's about thirty feet away, by that large rhododendron. He's a big man. Let me get the glasses on him.' There was a pause, then she spoke again. 'I thought so. It's MacGregor, Chief.'

'Has he got a spade or any tools with him?' Walsh asked.

'Can't see any.'

'Wait and see what he gets up to.'

175

Ten minutes later Brenda reported that MacGregor was now lying down, having wriggled under the lower branches of the rhododendron.

'Keep him under observation,' Walsh instructed.

Shortly after that, headquarters came in on their radio frequency with a message.

'A Professor Hughes has just rung in, wanting you, Chief Inspector. He wants to tell you that a chap called MacGregor is not in his room, and neither is his car where it usually is.'

Walsh grunted an acknowledgement.

That shrewd old professor had apparently kept an open mind, in spite of his conviction of MacGregor's innocence.

Now MacGregor was here, at the site. If he shortly came out of cover to destroy the archaeological evidence in trench 'K', then his denial that the tablet was planted as a practical joke would clearly be a lie. The University would kick the boy out in disgrace for that, and he, Walsh, would redouble the pressure on Forensic to find some tangible proof of MacGregor's presence in Lignum's house. That, with Fairbrother's statement that she was left alone in the punt, even for a short while, might be enough to convince a judge and jury that MacGregor was a killer.

However, the boy had made no move yet, and until he did so there were other possibilities that could not be completely discounted – although they needed an awful lot of ifs and buts to make any kind of a sensible scenario.

The weather forecast had been right. After midnight the cloud began to break up, bringing occasional glimpses of stars and the moon.

It was an hour later before one of the team had anything of significance to report.

'A car's just pulled in on the grass verge,' said the main road watcher, in a voice utterly devoid of emotion.

There was no need for any comment to be made on that sparse piece of information, and so the waiting continued, but with all the watchers now tense and wide awake.

'Calling headquarters. A car number check please,' and the watcher read out a sequence of letters and numbers.

176

The reply came quickly, certainly in less than a minute. 'It's a hire car. We're making further inquiries.'

The watcher spoke again, quietly and calmly. 'The driver is the only visible occupant. He's out of the car now, and opening the boot. He's taken out a spade, I think. Yes! It is a spade. Now he's jumped the ditch and is searching for a gap in the hedge. He looks like our man.'

'I can see him now,' Arthur Bryant's voice whispered excitedly. 'He's walking in as bold as brass. I don't think he's a clue that anyone's watching him.'

Through the night glasses Walsh could see him as well. He was a man of a little less than six feet tall, and of medium build.

At first he appeared to be heading directly towards the wooden hut, but a spoil heap near the first excavated area diverted him from his course, and he needed to use a torch to find a way round. When he was nearer the hut he stopped, and the torch was shone on to a sheet of paper. Clearly he had a site plan of the area, for subsequently the beam of the torch was used like a long white finger to identify the places marked. That beam eventually came to rest on trench 'K', and the figure moved towards it. He was obviously a careful man, because he then stopped again to check that he'd identified the right place.

Apparently he was now satisfied, for, with the spade still in one hand, he bent to unhook the tarpaulin loops from their pegs.

'All right! Start closing in on him. Take it nice and steady. We've plenty of time,' Walsh instructed, and he rose to his feet.

But he'd forgotten that there was one person close by who was not equipped to hear his instructions.

Brenda soon reminded him.

'MacGregor's on his feet, and he's going in, Chief,' she warned quickly.

'Hell and damnation!' Walsh muttered. 'Hold it, everyone. Stay still. Let's see what happens.'

Sure enough, the tall broad-shouldered young man was striding boldly across the turf, straight towards the intruder at trench 'K'.

Was this a planned meeting?

Walsh was soon to find out.

'What the hell do you think you're playing at?' MacGregor shouted, when he was only a few feet away from the trench.

The other man was clearly startled by the unexpected interruption, for he appeared to jump into the air in fright, but he recovered his composure and swung round with commendable alacrity.

'What the devil's that to do with you, mate? Bugger off, or you'll get hurt,' the intruder snarled, his voice a mixture of fear, anger and aggression, and to back up the threat he grasped the spade firmly in both hands and raised it shoulder-high.

MacGregor hesitated, very wisely, for that spade's blade shone silver in the moonlight, and it was clearly a formidable weapon, if used like a battleaxe, and that was the obvious intention.

In the young, though, wisdom is often swamped by the impetuousness of fearless bravery, and so it was in this case.

MacGregor moved forward again, but slowly and warily this time.

'I'll get hurt, will I?' he challenged. 'I don't think so. I don't know who you are, but I'm taking you to the police. I think you're the murderer of Sir Gordon Lignum.'

'I'm warning you. Don't be a bloody idiot. I'll use this if I have to,' the other snarled viciously, but he took a step backwards as he swung that glittering blade in a sweeping arc before him.

MacGregor took another purposeful step forward, but this time it was also slightly to one side.

'Close in now, quickly,' Walsh snapped into his radio.

That fool boy was getting dangerously close to that spade, Walsh thought, as he started hurrying forward. A blow from that might sever an arm, a leg, or a head.

MacGregor, however impetuous, was no fool; he had a plan. If he could force the spade-wielder back one pace more, that would be over the edge of trench 'K'. That would give him a good chance to overpower and disarm the man.

Unfortunately the intruder seemed to be aware of the danger; he suddenly stepped forward, swinging the spade like a scythe at MacGregor's legs.

MacGregor leaped back nimbly enough, but his heel caught a peg in the ground, and it was he who lost his balance and toppled backwards.

'Aha!' the intruder shouted in satisfaction, and stepped forward to administer the first and final blow of the contest.

Walsh sprinted forward and shouted to try and distract the prospective victor from making that final fatal stroke, but it began to look as though he would be too late.

Then another dark shadow sped into view from his right. It leapt the corner of the trench and dived forward with arms outstretched, to crash-land on the intruder's back. The two reeled about together for a moment, then Reg Finch came charging in like a Formula One bulldozer, and, with a heart-rending ripping of torn canvas, all three fell into the darkness of trench 'K'.


'I think you did very well indeed, Arthur,' Brenda said in a voice that was sufficiently tinged with envy and admiration to cause the recipient of such praise to lift up his head from his hands, and stare at her with mild astonishment. He was more used to admonishments and sarcasm from that source.

'Are you all right, Arthur?' Walsh demanded anxiously.

Arthur nodded. 'I will be in a minute, sir. I took a hell of a crack on my head,' he explained.

'I don't understand where you all suddenly came from. I thought I was here entirely on my own,' the bewildered Andrew MacGregor said rather breathlessly.

'It's a good thing you weren't on your own,' Reg Finch told him bluntly, 'or we might have had another murder on our hands.'

'Yes, I wasn't as clever as I thought I was,' MacGregor admitted, 'but to give him his due, I don't think he was out to kill me. He was trying to knock me out with the flat of his spade. Who on earth is he anyway?' MacGregor went on, pointing a finger at the intruder, now handcuffed, yet still held firmly by Alison.

'That man', Walsh announced with a smile, 'is the titular heir of the ninth baronet, so that makes him the tenth. Meet the murdered man's New Zealand cousin, Sir Adrian Lignum.'

'Good Lord!' MacGregor exclaimed. 'Do you mean to say that he killed his own cousin?'

'I didn't say that. In fact, I'm quite positive that he didn't, not unless the Wellington police are a load of dunderheads, and I'm sure they're not. Sir Adrian was in New Zealand at the time of his cousin's death, and therefore has a perfect alibi.'

'That's right, and so I was. You're not going to pin anything on me, Inspector.' Sir Adrian, now obviously recovered from his shock, was sounding much more like a solicitor.

'You think I can't pin anything on you?' Walsh said almost cheerfully. 'How about trespass, attempting to rob an archaeological site, and the attempted murder of young MacGregor here, for starters.'

'That's utter nonsense. I was out here minding my own business when I was attacked without provocation. I was defending myself. I demand to be released immediately, or you'll be in trouble, Inspector.'

'Chief,' Brenda interrupted these unproductive counter-accusations. 'Come over here and have a look at this.' She was holding the plan of the site that Sir Adrian had brought with him.

'It's beautifully done, isn't it?' she went on, holding her torch so that Walsh could see it clearly.

'So it is. It's almost a work of art,' Walsh agreed. 'That little sketch of the hut . . .'

'Lady Lignum,' Arthur muttered helpfully, still holding his head. 'She's an artist, isn't she?'

Walsh nodded and smiled.

'Take Sir Adrian to headquarters, and keep him in a cell for a while,' he said to the two uniformed officers who had appeared on the scene. 'We'll question him later. Now,

Arthur, we're going to take you, and your broken head, to Addenbrooke's Hospital. Maybe they'll tell us that you've had some sense knocked into it at last. Then we might spend some time there having a cup of coffee and chatting to people. In fact, who knows what we might get up to?'

Walsh felt quite surprised at this lighthearted feeling of jocularity, but then, some things about the strange case of the murder of Sir Gordon Lignum were beginning to make sense at last.


# 17


The overnight broken cloud had blown away, and day-break came with clear blue skies and a gentle invigoratingly cool breeze from the east.

It had all the signs of becoming a lovely day, especially for those active in mind and body.

Soon the devotees of the golf courses would be getting into the swing of things, and activity would begin on the tennis courts and the bowling greens. The River Cam would become crowded with punts and canoes going in all directions; for others, there were gardens to be attended to, cars to be washed and even windows to be cleaned.

To get the best out of such a promising day, it was always wise to make a good early start. At eight o'clock that morning, that was just what Walsh and his team set out to do, but perhaps they were a little too early.

'Brenda, you go round the back to the left. Reg, you go to the right,' Walsh directed with a wave of his arm. 'I'll give you a couple of minutes, then we'll go in.'

The front door was eventually opened a cautious fraction, by the frowning, lean-faced, grey-haired woman.

'I don't care if you are the police with a warrant. What kind of time is this to come visiting? I don't know if she's even dressed yet. You can come back later,' she cried out shrilly in answer to Walsh's request, while using her scrawny body as a door-stop to resist the pressure of the hand Walsh was using to try and push the door open wide enough to admit him.

'This isn't a social visit, damn it. This is official police business. Let us in,' Walsh growled angrily, giving the door a harder shove with his shoulder.

'Help!' the grey-haired woman screeched as she was forced to yield a few inches.

Then there were other excited voices, younger voices, in the hallway. Reinforcements had obviously come to aid the old woman to repel intruders, for the door ceased to move at all despite Walsh's increased pressure.

'Who do they want this time?' a girl asked.

'She's in the bathroom, I think,' another answered.

'Hey! You lot upstairs. Get your knickers on and come and help. We're being raided,' one of those girlish voices yelled out.

'Who needs knickers if we're all going to get ravished and raped anyway!'

'Are we? Me first. Let them in, let them in,' came the voice of another, who was barely able to talk for giggling.

'Bloody hell!' Walsh exclaimed wildly in frustration. He took a few seconds to try and think of different courses of action, but there weren't any – except to retreat. So he stepped back from the door suddenly, allowing it to slam shut. He hoped those inside had all fallen flat on their faces.

'Access to the house – not achieved,' he snapped out angrily into his radio. 'Block all rear exits.'

Brenda Phipps and Reg Finch were well positioned to carry out that instruction. They were in the narrow passage that serviced the back entrances of that row of houses and those of the adjoining street. It was high-fenced on both sides, though, and the gates were not numbered, so it was difficult to be quite sure which was the back entrance to the house in question. They were not in doubt for long. A first-floor frosted-glass bathroom sash window was squeakily pushed up. Reg peered through a gap in the slats of the fence and saw a long-legged, slim young woman, wearing scanty white knickers and little else, wriggle out and drop lightly on to the slated outhouse roof beneath. She held a bundle of clothes in her left arm, which was bandaged just above her wrist.

She walked gingerly to the end of the sloping roof, then leapt lightly across the four-foot gap to balance precariously on the top of the fence, preparing, presumably, to drop down into the passage. It was then that she saw the two upturned faces of the waiting police officers. She gave a shrill cry of dismay, and jumped instead right over the passage to the top of the fence opposite and then disappeared out of sight, into the garden of that house.

Reg rattled the gate, but it was bolted on the inside. So he set about scrambling over to follow the girl directly. Brenda, meanwhile, had turned and was running back down the passage, and at the same time yelling a warning into her radio.

Reg charged up the short path to the still-swinging back door of the house, and into the kitchen.

'Excuse me,' he said to the young man sitting there eating breakfast as he dashed through.

'I like it. Can anyone join in?' he heard the young man respond.

Reg did not reply, but ran down the dark passage, brushing past the hanging coats to the front hall, and thence out into the next street.

The girl had turned right, and was sprinting down the middle of the road, like some lithe-limbed athlete on a running track. However, she was heading straight towards a dark-clothed young man with a bandage round his head. That young man was already assuming the strange half-crouching position which a goalkeeper adopts when an attacker runs towards him with a ball at his feet.

The girl had quite clearly seen him, she could hardly have failed to, but she continued to run straight at him. At what seemed the very last moment she feinted her slender body to the left, but then quickly swerved to the right. It was a move of which any fleet-footed rugby wing threequarter might have been proud, and it so very nearly succeeded.

Arthur Bryant's diving hands could find no grip on the smooth soft flesh of the girl's waist, but one of his fingers did just manage to hook into the top of her skimpy white knickers, and it was those, when brought to her ankles, that actually caused her to trip and fall, so allowing the elusive white-skinned, dark-haired Australian girl to be captured.

'Really, Arthur, you mustn't go around pulling girls' knickers down in public,' Brenda murmured, as the police car drove away with their captive, now more suitably attired. 'I know the Chief's got into the habit of pulling Molly O'Brien's bra off whenever he sees her, but that's no excuse. It could get you into a whole lot of trouble.'

Arthur's face creased into a broad grin.

'It's all right to do it in private, is it?' he asked cheerfully.

Walsh smiled. Arthur's experiences that night seemed to have given him a lot more confidence. That was worth bearing in mind when the decision on his future had to be made.

'Right! We'll go and see how Forensic are getting on searching that girl's room, if they've managed to get past those blasted women. You want to go and see that trench being excavated, do you, Reg? Well, I don't see why not. We can meet up later on when Brenda and I get back from North London. There's no great hurry. I rather think it's all cut and dried now.'

It was late afternoon when Walsh and Brenda Phipps were directed by an Addenbrooke's staff nurse to a small lounge area at the far end of the main ward.

It was a cheerful airy room, with some large garish pictures on the white walls and several vases of bright flowers on the wide windowsills. It contained a motley collection of easy chairs, only one of which was occupied, by a dark-skinned girl in a silky dressing-gown of rich vibrant colours.

Melissa Fairbrother was obviously sufficiently well recovered from her injury to be allowed out of her bed, and now reclined in a chair by an open window. A small table beside her contained magazines and books, but it appeared she had no need of them, for she lay back relaxed and apparently watching out for visitors.

The two who had just arrived were not expected, or particularly welcome, judging from the momentary look of apprehension on her face.

'You appear to be recovering well,' Walsh said with a smile, after the initial greetings.

'Yes,' she replied seriously. 'Another two or three days, when they're sure there are no complications, then I can go out, provided I take things easily.'

'That's excellent,' Walsh announced quietly. 'Well, we've just popped in to give you some news. There have been some developments in the case we've been investigating, and I can now tell you that we are satisfied that neither you nor your friend Andrew are involved in any way.'

She blinked momentarily, then her serious expression gradually changed into one of animated youthful delight.

Walsh's news accounted for much of that reaction, but the rest of it was due to the arrival of some more visitors.

Andrew MacGregor was with a smiling Professor Hughes, who was carrying a large bunch of flowers and a box of chocolates. Reg Finch brought up the rear, accompanied by an elderly narrow-faced man, whom Walsh had never seen before.

'Tiny!' Melissa cried out, waving her hands expressively. 'The Chief Inspector says that we're both in the clear. We've nothing to worry about any more. Hello, Professor Hughes, isn't that wonderful news? Oh, what lovely flowers, thank you so very much.'

Andrew MacGregor sat down on the chair beside her, his smiling face looking surprisingly youthful today.

'I never doubted it for one moment,' he managed to chip in, but now Melissa was in full verbal flood. It was as though the news had breached some literary dam, and her pent-up words could come pouring out.

'It was half-past three this morning, when the Inspector came and woke me up, Tiny,' she exclaimed excitedly. 'The night staff were furious, as you'd imagine, but they didn't dare show it, did they? Not to the head of the CID, working on a murder case. He wanted to know all about Judy. You know, that Australian girl who's on the same landing as me. How long she'd been there. What car she drove. All that sort of thing.' She paused for breath.

The others were already seated, so Walsh pulled over a chair for himself, to complete a pleasantly intimate little circle.

'She's not an Australian, as a matter of fact,' Walsh informed her. 'That accent was just put on. She's a New Zealander from Wellington, and her name's not Judy either, but Kate – Kate Bottomley. Well, that's her maiden name, the one that's still on her passport and by which she's known in North London, but until a few days ago her real name was Mrs Katherine Lignum. Now she's a Lady – Lady Katherine Lignum, Sir Adrian Lignum's wife.'

Walsh's words, not unexpectedly, created an interestingly vibrant silence, as their meaning was being mentally absorbed. Naturally the quickest at that sort of thing was Professor Hughes.

'Was Sir Gordon's murder premeditated then?' Hughes asked, frowning deeply, because obviously the picture he had formed in his mind seemed flawed in some way.

Walsh shrugged his shoulders.

'Probably,' he acknowledged. 'Kate Bottomley came to London at the end of last year, to study for some art diploma or other, and took rooms in North London, but she married Adrian Lignum in a registry office in Christchurch, New Zealand first. If murder was in her mind, then clearly she wasn't prepared to commit it unless she was absolutely certain that she gained all the rewards. They kept very quiet about the wedding, for obvious reasons. Anyway, it was as Kate Bottomley that she came to London. Once here she spent much of her spare time in Cambridge, without ever introducing herself to her cousin-in-law Sir Gordon, but she certainly made the effort to find out as much as she could about him, even to the extent of becoming acquainted with some of his archaeological students. No doubt it was from them, talking among themselves, that she learned all about the finding of the cuneiform tablet, and Sir Gordon's reaction to it.'

'The thought of disposing of Sir Gordon really must have been firmly fixed in her mind,' Brenda stated positively, 'but only if she could be pretty certain that someone else would take the blame. I think she thought that the business over the cuneiform tablet could, with a bit of help, be turned into a good motive for murder, with Melissa and Andrew as the obvious suspects.'

'But why? What would she get out of it, other than a title?' Andrew asked.

'There's a fair income from a pretty substantial trust fund that goes with the title, but I think the title itself was the big attraction for her,' Reg Finch explained. 'As Lady Katherine, she probably saw herself becoming a social celebrity in New Zealand, and moving in the uppermost circles.'

'Possibly she would have, too,' Walsh said seriously. 'It's amazing what a title can do to a career. Even after only a few days of becoming the new Sir Adrian Lignum, he was being approached about partnerships and directorships.'

'She was taking a big risk though, wasn't she? What if one of us met her in later life and recognised her as the Judy we'd known in Cambridge?' Melissa asked.

Walsh smiled and shook his head. 'She'd thought of that. The Judy you knew had dark hair and dark eyes. Kate Bottomley has fair hair and blue eyes. She'd dyed her hair, you see, and when in Cambridge wore specially tinted contact lenses with dark make-up for her eyebrows. Back in London, while doing her art course, she wore a fair-haired wig – we found that in her car. A simple disguise, and an effective one. Anyway, having decided that there was an opportunity to commit murder and cast the blame fairly and squarely on someone else, Kate Bottomley got herself digs in the same house as you, Melissa, under the false name of Judy, making herself out to be an Australian and a student at one of the language schools. There she was nicely at the centre of things, and could do her best to make sure suspicion fell on you and

Andrew. You girls chatter away to each other much too easily, Melissa. You must have mentioned taking photos on the site, so Kate stole your camera, and you must have talked to her about your planned punt trip up the Cam with Andrew. Kate knew it would take you past the end of Sir Gordon's back garden, and that was her big opportunity. That night she climbed over the side gate to the back of Sir Gordon's house, and found him alone, working at his desk while listening to music that would drown any sounds that she might make creeping up behind him. What could be better for someone with an evil intent in mind? So she killed him.'

'Does she admit that?' the professor asked in surprise.

'No,' Walsh smiled ruefully, 'but she does admit to hitting him with something heavy that happened to be lying on his desk. That, she says, was in self-defence. Her story is that when she called to introduce herself as his cousin's wife, Sir Gordon became sexually aroused and tried to rape her.'

'Nonsense! Sir Gordon would never have done a thing like that,' Melissa said indignantly.

'Her story doesn't fit with the forensic evidence either, or explain why she then went on to rob the house. Never mind, as she expected, we quickly had you two on our suspect list, and she set about trying to keep you there. She dug up trench "K", feeling certain that we would think Andrew had done it, and she took the items she'd stolen from Sir Gordon's house to a fence, whose name she'd read in a local North London newspaper, near where she had her other flat. She left a note with the stolen items signed A.M., to make us think it was young Andrew here.'

'We wasted a lot of time watching that fence's house in Enfield, waiting for A.M. to turn up,' Reg Finch added, 'but it was when she heard Melissa admit to me that Andrew had left her for a short while, that night on the punt, that she decided it might now be in order for Andrew to murder his accomplice, obviously to prevent any more such revelations. Hence the knife attack on you, Melissa, which fortunately went wrong. I think she pulled her windcheater up over her head when she approached you in that passageway. That

188

would make her look bigger than she was, and might account for you thinking your attacker had no head. However, when you flung out your hand to protect yourself, you whacked her sufficiently hard to crack a small bone in her left forearm. It must have hurt if she tried to do anything strenuous, that's why she had to bring her husband in on the next part of her plan to provide even more circumstantial evidence against Andrew, which was digging up the extended trench "K".'

'To make sure he dug in the right place, she had to draw him a map of the site, and probably without thinking, her pencil made it into a little work of art. In one place she drew a little hut that's so good it seems to stand out of the paper, just like that sketch she did of you, Melissa. That rather gave her game away,' Walsh explained.

'How did you find out who she really was?' Melissa asked.

Walsh smiled grimly. 'At half-past three this morning you told me which was her car. She'd bought that in North London, and it was registered in her real name. Bringing it to Cambridge was a mistake, but she needed it, of course, because she had to drive down to attend her art classes each day. We spent the rest of the early hours of this morning telephoning New Zealand, to discover the link between Kate Bottomley and Adrian Lignum. Fortunately it was daytime over there, and they were very helpful.'

'So, all's well that ends well,' Professor Hughes exclaimed philosophically. 'Now we have some exciting news for you too, Melissa. Trench "K" has yielded some more fragments of cuneiform tablets. Oh yes,' he went on, beaming in delight at Melissa's expression of astonishment. 'You may not know my friend, Professor Durrant, here,' and he waved an arm to introduce the elderly narrow-faced man. 'He's an Assyriologist from Trinity. He can read those tablets as easily as you can read a book in English.'

Professor Durrant smiled shyly. 'It's all very interesting, this, I'm sure. However, surprisingly enough, when one has recovered from the initial shock of the discovery, it really is no great earth-shattering find, I'm sorry to say,' he said, rather nervously shuffling a few coloured photographs of tablet fragments in his hands. 'There were obviously several different tablets, and they're very incomplete. Hittite, of course,' he went on, as though that fact should have been obvious to all those there. 'They appear to be simple prayers to their gods, exhorting special protection, for some reason.'

'I can add to your collection,' Walsh interrupted with a smile, and reached forward to hand Durrant another large coloured photograph. 'That, presumably, is the original tablet that Melissa dug up. We'll have to hang on to it for a while, because it's a vital piece of evidence. We found it in Kate Bottomley's room in North London. It might seem strange that she should have hung on to such an incriminating item, but I think she kept it hoping for an opportunity to plant it in your room, Andrew. If she'd managed that, it would really have put you on the spot.'

Professor Durrant wasn't interested in such speculation, though; he had almost snatched at the new photograph, and was peering at it intently.

'Now this is much more interesting,' he mumbled to himself. 'This is a letter asking aid and protection for an expedition to find the Sun Goddess of Arinna.' He blinked and shook his head, allowing long strands of white hair to fall over his forehead. He brushed them away.

'You know, Edwin, I think we might find all these come from King Mursili, at the time of the Hittite plague. It lasted nigh on twenty years, if you remember, and Mursili nearly went out of his mind exhorting the gods to lift the curse from his land and people.' He scratched vigorously at his head just above his left ear. 'It would make sense, you know. To find the Sun Goddess, an expedition would have had to travel westward, into the setting sun. That was the direction of her home, you see, where she went at night, during the hours of darkness. There are hints of such expeditions in other texts, and of course, one must remember that the Egyptians were great explorers too.'

'You mean those Hittites may have travelled all the way here, from what is now Turkey, professor?' Brenda asked.

'There's no reason why they shouldn't,' Professor Hughes interrupted. 'Mind you, Ireland is further west than here. They may have got that far, and found there was no way they could go further. So they might even have been on their way home. Fascinating, isn't it?'

'What do you think happened to them in the end?' Melissa asked.

'Dr Choosely is of the opinion that they may have built themselves a small wooden fort to pass the winter in, and that it got burnt down. Whether by accident or by hostile action, we'll probably never know,' Reg Finch explained.

'That would account for the thick layer of carboniferous material,' Andrew added, nodding wisely. 'It's a bit of an anticlimax, really, having it all explained as simply as that.'

'It was pure good luck, us finding it,' Melissa reflected happily.

'That piece of good luck, as you put it, Melissa,' Reg Finch ventured, 'resulted in you being put nearly at the top of a murder suspect list, and coming close to being a victim yourself.'

'Near the top? You made me feel right at the top, on my own,' Melissa replied bitterly, failing utterly to respond to the friendly smile of her one-time tormentor.

Reg shrugged his shoulders ruefully. 'At times you were equal first, with Andrew, and a whole clubful of motor cyclists.'

Melissa looked surprised, and a little mollified. 'I wish I'd known that at the time. It might have made things easier to bear.'

'Never mind,' Professor Hughes beamed, reaching forward to give Melissa's hand a fatherly pat. 'All that is now behind you. Forget it, and start looking forward to the future again. You made a little piece of history when your trowel exposed that tablet to the light of day, after nearly four thousand years, and I think that should be acknowledged. I do have some influence in this University, and I shall insist that henceforth these tablets should be known as the Fairbrother Tablets. There! What do you think of that?'

191

Melissa and Andrew looked at each other with bright intelligent smiling eyes.

Clearly, Brenda thought, their shared experiences over the past few days had brought forth a strong bond of friendship and trust between them. Whether that bond would develop into deeper and stronger feelings of love and affection, neither of them knew. What they both clearly wanted was to be left alone together, so they could start the process of finding out. However, their visitors would leave soon enough and they had time in abundance.

So Melissa smiled politely at the still-beaming Professor Hughes.

'The Fairbrother Tablets, professor? I say, thank you very much, that would be very nice,' she said hesitantly, then started giggling out of sheer happiness.